OPENING NIGHT, MARCH 31, 1977

The Morosco Theatre

**Operated by the L-O Management Corporation,
Lester Osterman — Richard Horner — Allan Francis**

**Lester Osterman, Ken Marsolais, Allan Francis
and Leonard Soloway**

present

The Mark Taper Forum/Long Wharf Theatre

production of

THE SHADOW BOX

*1977 Tony Award Winner
1977 Pulitzer Prize Winner*

by

MICHAEL CRISTOFER

*starring
(in alphabetical order)*

JOYCE EBERT	**PATRICIA ELLIOTT**
GERALDINE FITZGERALD	**ROSE GREGORIO**
LAURENCE LUCKINBILL	**SIMON OAKLAND**
MANDY PATINKIN	**JOSEF SOMMER**

VINCENT STEWART

Setting by	*Costumes by*	*Lighting by*
MING CHO LEE	**BILL WALKER**	**RONALD WALLACE**

Directed by

GORDON DAVIDSON

Originally produced by Center Theatre Group of Los Angeles
at the Mark Taper Forum.

LONG WHARF THEATRE:
Arvin Brown, Artistic Director; M. Edgar Rosenblum, Executive Director

CENTER THEATRE GROUP:
Gordon Davidson, Artistic Director; William P. Wingate, General Manager

Associate Producers: Philip Getter and Bernard Stuchin

THE CAST
(in order of appearance)

THE INTERVIEWER .... *Josef Sommer*

COTTAGE ONE

JOE .... *Simon Oakland*

STEVE .... *Vincent Stewart*

MAGGIE .... *Joyce Ebert*

COTTAGE TWO

BRIAN .... *Laurence Luckinbill*

MARK .... *Mandy Patinkin*

BEVERLY .... *Patricia Elliott*

COTTAGE THREE

AGNES .... *Rose Gregorio*

FELICITY .... *Geraldine Fitzgerald*

The play takes place in three cottages on the grounds of a large hospital.

4

THE SHADOW BOX

A DRAMA IN TWO ACTS

by Michael Cristofer

SAMUEL FRENCH, INC.

45 WEST 25TH STREET   NEW YORK 10010

7623 SUNSET BOULEVARD   HOLLYWOOD 90046

LONDON   *TORONTO*

"There are five different stages that a person will go through when he faces the fact of his own death: denial, anger, bargaining, depression, and acceptance. These stages will last for different periods of time, they will replace each other, or exist at times side by side . . . But the one thing that usually persists through all these stages is hope."

E. Kubler-Ross, M.D.

CHARACTERS

COTTAGE ONE:

JOE

MAGGIE

STEVE

COTTAGE TWO:

BRIAN

MARK

BEVERLY

COTTAGE THREE:

FELICITY

AGNES

INTERVIEWER

The Shadow Box

ACT ONE

Morning.

A small cottage that looks like a vacation house, set in the trees, secluded. A front porch, a living room area, and a large kitchen area.

The lights come up first on a small area Downstage and away from the cottage. We will call this area the "Interview Area."

JOE *is surprised by the light. He is a strong, thick-set man, a little bit clumsy with moving and talking, but full of energy.*

He steps into the light and looks out toward the back of the theatre. A MIKED VOICE speaks to him.

VOICE OF INTERVIEWER. Joe? Joe, can you hear me?
JOE. Huh? (*Looking around.*) What . . . uh . . . ?
VOICE OF INTERVIEWER. Can you hear me?
JOE. Oh, yeah. Sure. I can hear you real good.
VOICE OF INTERVIEWER. Good. Have a seat, Joe.
JOE. (*Still looking around, a little amused.*) What?
Hey, where . . . uh . . . I can't see . . .
VOICE OF INTERVIEWER. We're out here.
JOE. What? Oh, yeah. I get it.
VOICE OF INTERVIEWER. Yes.
JOE. You can see me. Right?
VOICE OF INTERVIEWER. Yes. That's correct.

JOE. You can see me, but I . . .

VOICE OF INTERVIEWER. Yes.

JOE. . . . can't see you. Yeah. (*He laughs.*) I get it now. You can *see* me, huh?

VOICE OF INTERVIEWER. Yes, we can.

JOE. Far out.

VOICE OF INTERVIEWER. What?

JOE. (*Smiling.*) Nothing. Nothing. Well, how do I look?

VOICE OF INTERVIEWER. Have a seat, Joe.

JOE. That bad, huh? I *feel* all right. Lost a little weight, but outside of that . . .

VOICE OF INTERVIEWER. Have a seat, Joe.

JOE. Sure, sure. (*He sits.*) Okay. What?

VOICE OF INTERVIEWER. Nothing special. We just wanted to talk. Give you a chance to see how we do this.

JOE. Sure. You got people watching, huh?

VOICE OF INTERVIEWER. Yes. There's nothing very complicated about it. It's just a way for us to stay in touch.

JOE. Yeah. It's like being on T.V.

VOICE OF INTERVIEWER. Just relax.

JOE. Right. Fire away.

VOICE OF INTERVIEWER. You seem to be in very good spirits.

JOE. Never better. Like I said, I feel great.

VOICE OF INTERVIEWER. Good. (*There is a pause.* JOE *looks out into the lights.*)

JOE. My family is coming today.

VOICE OF INTERVIEWER. Yes. We know.

JOE. It's been a long time. Almost six months. They would have come sooner, but we couldn't afford it. Not after all these goddamn bills. And then I always figured I'd be going home. I always figured I'd get myself back into shape and . . . (*Pause.*)

VOICE OF INTERVIEWER. Have you seen the cottage?

JOE. Yeah. Yeah, it's real nice. It's beautiful. They're going to love it.

VOICE OF INTERVIEWER. Good.

JOE. Maggie always wanted a place in the mountains. But I'm an ocean man. So, every summer, we always ended up at the beach. She liked it all right. It just takes her a while to get used to things. She'll love it here, though. She will. It's real nice.

VOICE OF INTERVIEWER. Good.

JOE. It just takes her a little time.

(*The lights slowly start to come up on the cottage area.* MAGGIE *and* STEVE'S VOICES *are heard Offstage.*)

STEVE. Here. Over here.

MAGGIE. Stephen!

VOICE OF INTERVIEWER. (*To* JOE.) Then everything is settled, right?

JOE. Oh, yeah. Maggie knows the whole setup. I wrote to her.

VOICE OF INTERVIEWER. And your son?

JOE. Steve? Yeah. I told Maggie to tell him. I figured he should know before he got here.

VOICE OF INTERVIEWER. Good.

JOE. It's not an easy thing.

STEVE. (*Still Offstage—overlapping.*) Come on, Mom.

JOE. I guess you know that.

MAGGIE. (*Still Offstage.*) Give me a chance to catch my breath.

JOE. You get used to the idea, but it's not easy.

VOICE OF INTERVIEWER. You seem fine.

JOE. Oh, me. Yeah, sure. But Maggie . . .

MAGGIE. (*Overlapping.*) What number did you say it was?

VOICE OF INTERVIEWER. (*Overlapping.*) What number cottage are you in?

JOE. Uh . . . one. Number one.

STEVE. (*Overlapping.*) Number one. One, they said.

JOE. You get scared at first. Plenty. And then you get pissed off. Oh, is that all right to say.

VOICE OF INTERVIEWER. Yes, Joe. That's all right. It's all right for you to be angry or depressed or even happy . . . if that's how you feel. We want to hear as much as you want to tell us.

STEVE. (*Still Offstage.*) Look at all these goddamn trees!

MAGGIE. (*Still Off.*) Watch your mouth.

JOE. Yeah, cause I was. Plenty pissed off. I don't mind telling you that. In fact, I'm glad just to say it. You get tired of keeping it all inside. But it's like, nobody wants to hear about it. You know what I mean? Even the doctors . . . they shove a thermometer in your mouth and a stethoscope in their ears. . . . How the hell are you supposed to say anything? But then, like I said, you get used to it . . . I guess . . .

STEVE. Come on, Mom!

JOE. There's still a few things . . .

MAGGIE. You're going to give me a heart attack.

JOE. I could talk to you about them . . . maybe later.

VOICE OF INTERVIEWER. Even if it's just to listen. That's what we're here for, Joe.

JOE. I mean, it happens to everybody, right? I ain't special.

VOICE OF INTERVIEWER. I guess not Joe.

JOE. I mean, that's the way I figure it. We could talk about that, too.

VOICE OF INTERVIEWER. Yes, we can.

JOE. Maybe tomorrow.

VOICE OF INTERVIEWER. Alright, Joe. We won't keep you now.

JOE. I'm a little nervous today.

VOICE OF INTERVIEWER. But if you need anything . . .

JOE. (*Distracted.*) Huh . . . What . . . ?

VOICE OF INTERVIEWER. If you need anything . . .

JOE. Oh, sure. Thanks. We'll be all right.

VOICE OF INTERVIEWER. You know where to find us.

JOE. Is that it?

VOICE OF INTERVIEWER. That's it. Unless *you* have something . . .

JOE. Oh . . . yeah. One thing . . . I . . . uh . . .

STEVE. (STEVE, *a young boy, about fourteen years old, enters.*) Dad? (*He rushes onto the stage, runs around the cottage.*)

MAGGIE. (*Still Offstage.*) Stephen?

STEVE. Here! Over here!

JOE. I . . . uh . . . no. No. I guess not.

VOICE OF INTERVIEWER. All right, then. Thank you, Joe.

JOE. Sure. Any time.

STEVE. (*Rushing into the cottage.*) Number one. This is it! Jesus!

JOE. Oh, yeah. I want to thank you for making all this possible. (*He looks out into the lights. There is no answer.*) Hello?

STEVE. He's not there.

JOE. You still there? (*Still no answer.*) Well, I'd better be getting back. (*Still no answer. The lights*

*fade on the Interview Area and come up full on the
cottage.*)

STEVE. (*Running out of the cottage.*) Mom? Where
the hell . . .

JOE. (*Turning toward the cottage.*) Stephen! Hey,
dad!

STEVE. Holy shit! Holy . . . ! (*He does a little
dance, runs to his Father and embraces him.*) Where
the hell . . .

JOE. There you are . . . I been waiting all day.

STEVE. . . . have you been? We been traipsing
around the whole goddamn place. . . .

JOE. (*Laughing.*) I been here. Waiting. Where's your
mother?

STEVE. One cottage after another. Is this it. Is this it.

MAGGIE. (*Still Off.*) Joe? Stephen, is that your
father?

STEVE. Far out! I brought my guitar. Wait till you
hear . . . (*Calling Off.*) Mom! Over here, for Christ's
sake. (*To* JOE.) So many goddamn trees . . .

JOE. What do you think? Huh?

STEVE. So many . . .

JOE. There's a bunk in there.

MAGGIE. (*Off.*) Joe?

JOE. Hey, Maggie. Get the lead out!

STEVE. Yeah. I saw. Bunk beds and a fireplace . . .
we got any wood?

JOE. You can take the top one night and the bottom
the next.

STEVE. Uh-uh. I'll take the bottom. I fall off, I'll
break my fucking head.

JOE. I'll break your fucking head, if you don't watch
your fucking mouth.

STEVE. Holy, holy shit! (STEVE *hugs his Father again.* JOE *holds him at arms length for a second, to catch his breath.*) You okay?

JOE. (*Quickly recovers and returns to his previous level of energy.*) Yeah, yeah. I'm great.

STEVE. You look terrific. I was worried. I missed you. Hey! How long can we stay? Huh?

JOE. (*Holding him tightly.*) I don't know. A couple of weeks . . . I don't know how long it . . .

STEVE. Great. (*He drags* JOE *into the cottage.*) Come on. I'll show you the guitar. It was pretty cheap. I ripped off the case, so that didn't cost anything. It's got a little compartment on the inside for picks and capos and dope and shit like that . . .

(*They go into the cottage.* MAGGIE *struggles onto the stage, a mass of bundles, shopping bags and suitcases. She's dressed up—high heels, bright yellow print dress—but she looks a mess. She's been walking too long, carrying too big a load. Finally, she stops near the cottage.*)

MAGGIE. End of the line. Everybody off. (*And she lets all the shopping bags, packages, and suitcases crash to the ground around her. She straightens her back with a groan and looks around her.*) Steve? Joe? The jackass is here! Come and get your luggage? (*No answer. She walks up to the porch of the cabin, and tentatively takes one step up. But the cottage seems to frighten her. She stops, looks at it and then backs away from it.*) You leave me alone out here for one more minute and I'm taking the next plane back to Newark. (*She gives out a long, loud whistle through her teeth.*) Stephen, are you in there or not?

STEVE. (*From inside the cottage.*) Hey, Mom, come on in if you're coming.

MAGGIE. I'm not coming in. You're coming out. And don't give me . . .

JOE. (*Coming out of the cottage and saying her line with her.*) . . . and don't give me any smart back talk or I'll split your lip.

(*Surprised by* JOE's *sudden appearance, she doesn't move for a second. Then, very carefully, she takes a few slow steps toward him.* JOE *walks down to meet her. All* MAGGIE *can manage to do is reach out one hand and touch him, just to see if he's really there. When she is sure that he's not an illusion, she takes a deep breath, goes back to her bundles, and starts talking very quickly, trying to keep control of herself.*)

MAGGIE. Well . . . I brought you some things . . . I didn't know what, what for sure you'd want, but I thought it was better to be sure, safe . . . so . . .

JOE. We'll take them inside . . .

MAGGIE. No . . . Steve'll get them. I been dragging them all . . .

JOE. Let me look at you, huh?

MAGGIE. (*Continues to fumble nervously with her hair, her dress, the packages.*) I didn't know what you'd need. There's some jelly and some peppers I put up. (*She starts pulling jars out of one of the bags.*) I thought it was forty pounds on the plane, but they let you have extra. You can put things under the seat. A lot of people didn't *have* anything, so I put stuff under *their* seats, too.

JOE. How are you, Maggie?

MAGGIE. Oh, fine, I brought the newspapers. (*She pulls more jars out.*) Some cookies, and some pumpkin flowers. The airplane made me sick. There was a man sitting next to me. He kept talking and talking. All those clouds. It looked like you could walk on them. I wanted to throw up, but the man next to me made me so nervous I couldn't. Where did I put . . .

JOE. Come on inside. You want some coffee?

MAGGIE. (*Reaching into another bag.*) I brought some coffee. You've got everything here already. You should've told me.

JOE. I did. I told you over the phone.

MAGGIE. I don't remember. I'll clean up tomorrow. First thing. Straighten everything out.

JOE. It's already clean.

MAGGIE. You want to live in somebody else's dirt?

JOE. Maggie, it isn't the Poconos. It's clean. It's clean.

MAGGIE. Well, you can't be too sure. Mom sent some bread . . .

JOE. How is she?

MAGGIE. Oh, good. Yeah. She fell down and hurt her leg. I don't know. It's not healing so good. She's getting old. What can you do. But she made the bread anyway. I told her not to, but she said she wanted to. So . . . And Fanny says hello. She gave me . . . uh, something . . .

JOE. I can see it later.

MAGGIE. . . . where is it? Oh, yeah. (*She pulls out a wrapped package.*) I don't know what it is. You know Fanny. It could be anything . . . and some clam broth. (*Takes out spilled clam broth.*) Oh, Pop and Josie, they went crabbing, they took the kids. Steve went with them. They gave me almost a whole

bushel. So I made some sauce. (*Another jar emerges.*)
We can . . . do you have a stove in there?

JOE. Sure. Come on inside. I'll show you. It's real
nice. (*He starts to head her toward the cottage, but
she pulls away.*)

MAGGIE. No, I don't want to go inside.

JOE. Huh? Why not?

MAGGIE. I don't . . . I'll see it. I'll see it.

JOE. But . . .

MAGGIE. How do I look? It's a new dress.

JOE. You look real pretty.

MAGGIE. I got dressed for the plane. I don't know.
I should have worn pants. You get so tired, sitting, all
pushed together like that. My ears hurt so bad. Steve
loved it. I couldn't make him sit still. He was all over
the place, taking pictures. The stewardess was crazy
about him. She was *pretty*, too. They look real nice.
They wear . . . they smile. I asked her what to do
about my ears and she just smiled. I don't think she
heard me. So I smiled, too, but it didn't do any
good . . .

JOE. (*Hugs her.*) You must be tired, huh?

MAGGIE. Yeah. I don't know.

JOE. Come on in. You can rest.

MAGGIE. (*Ignores his offer.*) One minute you're there.
The next minute you're here. I still feel like I'm there.
(*She pulls away from him and starts rummaging
through the bags.*) What else? Three thousand miles,
it must be. They . . . Oh, yeah. I made a ham . . .
(*She pulls the monster out of a bag.*)

JOE. What?

MAGGIE. A ham. We can have it for lunch.

JOE. Christ!

MAGGIE. What's the matter? It's no good?

JOE. You mean you carried a ham three thousand miles across the country?

MAGGIE. No. I put it under the seat.

JOE. Well, what the hell are we going to do with it?

MAGGIE. I don't know . . . I thought it'd last, so . . .

JOE. We *got* everything we need. I told you.

MAGGIE. I don't remember. You can't eat this, huh?

JOE. No, I can eat it. I can eat it. That's not what I'm talking about.

MAGGIE. Then what *are* you talking about?

JOE. I'm talking about they got ham in California. They got stores like everyplace in the world and you go in and you buy whatever you want . . .

MAGGIE. (*Making a vain effort to hide the ham.*) I'll take it back with me . . .

JOE. It's all right! It's here now.

MAGGIE. It'll keep. I'll put it away. You don't have to look at it.

JOE. No. It's fine. It's all right. What the hell are we talking about?

MAGGIE. (*All upset, still holding on to the ham.*) You didn't say in the letter. And we talked and I couldn't remember. I tried. What the hell. They said to come and bring Steve. That's all. At first I thought that was it. Then I got your letter and you sound fine and I talk to you . . . so, I made the ham, I . . . (*She cries. JOE goes to her. Holds her and the ham in his arms.*)

JOE. I missed you, Maggie. I missed you real bad. (*Hugs her.*)

MAGGIE. You got to tell me what's going on. Don't make me feel so stupid. Like I'm supposed to know

everything. I don't know anything. I just know what
I see.

JOE. Maggie . . .

MAGGIE. But you look real good. You're all right
now, huh?

JOE. Maggie, listen . . .

MAGGIE. No. It's all right. You don't have to tell
me. I can see it. You're fine. Huh? It's just I got so
scared. Thinking about it. Making things up in my
head. But it's all right now. I can see it's all right.
I knew it would be when I got here.

JOE. (*Giving in.*) Yes, Maggie. Everything's all
right.

MAGGIE. I knew it. I knew it.

(*They embrace, and move Upstage. Our focus shifts
now to the Interview Area.* BRIAN *is talking.*)

BRIAN. . . . people don't want to let go. Do they?

VOICE OF INTERVIEWER. How do you mean, Brian?

BRIAN. They think it's a mistake, they think it's
supposed to last forever. I'll never understand that.
My God, it's the one thing in this world you can be
sure of! No matter who you are, no matter what you
do, no matter anything—sooner or later—it's going to
happen. You're going to die. (BRIAN *is a graceful man
. . . simple, direct, straightforward . . . mind and
body balanced, like an athlete.*) . . . and that's a relief—if you think about it. I should say if you think
clearly about it.

VOICE OF INTERVIEWER. I'm not sure I follow you.

BRIAN. Well, the trouble is that most of us spend
our entire lives trying to *forget* that we're going to die.
And some of us even succeed. It's like pulling the cart

with*out* the horse. Or is that a poor analogy? (STEVE *enters and sits in woods with guitar.*)

VOICE OF INTERVIEWER. No, Brian. I think it's fine.

BRIAN. Well, you get the gist of it anyway. I'm afraid I've really lost my touch with words. They don't add up as neatly as they used to.

VOICE OF INTERVIEWER. But you're still writing.

BRIAN. Oh, yes. With great abandon. I may have lost touch with the words, but I still have faith in them. Eventually they have to mean *something* . . . give or take a few thousand monkeys, a few thousand typewriters. I'm not particular. Am I being helpful or just boring?

VOICE OF INTERVIEWER. Very helpful.

BRIAN. Well, I don't see how. Too much thinking and talking. My former wife once said to me, 'We've done enough thinking. Couldn't we just dance for a few years?'

VOICE OF INTERVIEWER. Did you?

BRIAN. No. I have lousy feet. Instead, I started going on about music and mathematics, the difference between Apollonian airs and Dionysian rites, explaining to her the history of dance and the struggle with form . . . and before I finished the first paragraph, she was gone . . .

(*The lights fade on the porch area of the cottage where* JOE *and* MAGGIE *are. Then they start to come up on the living room area of the cottage.* BRIAN *continues his interview.*)

VOICE OF INTERVIEWER. Gone for good?

BRIAN. Like a bat out of hell.

VOICE OF INTERVIEWER. I see.

BRIAN. So do I . . . now. But then I didn't. I became totally irrational . . . idiotic, in the Greek sense of the word. I blamed her, I damned her, I hated her . . . I missed her. And I got so worked up I began to realize what she was talking about. You see, I'd lost the energy of it, the magic of it. No wonder she left. After all, the universe isn't a syllogism, it's a miracle. Isn't it? And if you can believe in one small part of it, then you can believe in all of it. And if you can believe in all of it . . . well, that *is* a reason for dancing, isn't it?

VOICE OF INTERVIEWER. What happened to her?

BRIAN. Beverly? Oh, she's still dancing as far as I know.

VOICE OF INTERVIEWER. I see.

BRIAN. Well, every life makes sense on its own terms, I suppose. She must be very happy. I'm sure of that. Otherwise she would have come back. There I go, rambling on again. I'm sorry.

VOICE OF INTERVIEWER. You seem to have everything so well thought out.

(*In the living room area of the cottage,* MARK *enters. He is a young man, passionately intelligent, sexually attractive.*)

BRIAN. (*Still talking to the* INTERVIEWER.) Well, I think it's important to be sensible. Even about the miraculous. Otherwise you lose track of what it's all about.

VOICE OF INTERVIEWER. How is Mark? (MARK *enters.*)

BRIAN. (*Smiles.*) Speaking of the miraculous . . . Well, he's fine.

MARK. (*In the living room, looking around.*) Brian?

BRIAN. (*To* INTERVIEWER.) What's the official line on him now?

VOICE OF INTERVIEWER. How do you mean?

BRIAN. Well, I know these are supposed to be strictly family situations. I'm curious. I mean, what are we calling him this week? Nephew? Cousin? Butler?

VOICE OF INTERVIEWER. No. I have him down as a friend.

BRIAN. I see.

VOICE OF INTERVIEWER. In the Greek sense of the word.

BRIAN. (*Laughs.*) Very good. Very good.

VOICE OF INTERVIEWER. He's welcome to come and talk to us if he likes. (*In the living room area,* MARK *takes off his jacket, throws it on a chair, sits down and takes out a package . . .*)

BRIAN. Well, we've talked a lot about it already. Generally, we have the same opinion on the subject. Wisdom doesn't always come with age. Occasionally the young can be as rational as you or I. (MARK *carefully takes six or seven bottles of medication from the package. He makes notes of each label, copying down the information in a small pad.*)

VOICE OF INTERVIEWER. Yes. I suppose they can.

BRIAN. (*Checking his watch.*) My watch is stopped. How long have I been babbling?

VOICE OF INTERVIEWER. It doesn't matter. There's no hurry.

BRIAN. Not for you, maybe. Some of us are on a tighter schedule.

VOICE OF INTERVIEWER. I am sorry. I didn't mean . . .

BRIAN. (*Laughs.*) It's all right. It's all right. You

mustn't take all of this too seriously. I don't . . . Our
dreams are beautiful, our fate is sad. But day by day,
it's generally pretty funny. We can talk again tomorrow, if you want. I don't mind. It's a bit of a shock,
that's all. You always think . . . no matter what they
tell you . . . you always think you have more time.
And you don't. But I appreciate what you're trying
to do here, and I do enjoy being a guinea pig.

VOICE OF INTERVIEWER. Good. Very good.

BRIAN. Tomorrow, then. If I'm still breathing. Or
even if I'm not, I don't think it'll stop me from talking.

VOICE OF INTERVIEWER. Yes. Tomorrow.

(BRIAN *exits. The lights fade on the Interview Area
and come up on the living room.* MARK *puts the
medicine in a bookcase that is already loaded
with bottles of pills and boxes of medical supplies.*
BEVERLY *comes bursting into the living room,
blowing a party horn.*)

BEVERLY. Surprise! Oh, who are you? I'm sorry. I'm
looking for Brian . . . uh . . . Two. They said cottage two. I must have . . .

MARK. No, you didn't . . .

BEVERLY. I didn't?

MARK. No. This is two. This is cottage two.

BEVERLY. Oh.

MARK. Yes.

BEVERLY. Thank God. (*Pause.*) Is . . . uh . . .

MARK. (*A little uncomfortable.*) No. Not at the
moment. But he should be back any minute.

BEVERLY. Good. (*Another pause. They look at each
other.*) I wanted to surprise him and he's not here.
Well . . . surprise! (BEVERLY *starts to walk around*

ACT I THE SHADOW BOX 23

the cottage. She is an extremely attractive woman. Middle-aged. She's dressed curiously in what was once a very expensive, chic evening dress. But it is now soiled and torn. She also has over and around the dress about twenty odd pieces of jewelry attached wherever there is room for them. In her hand a noise-maker that squeaks uncheerfully, and over everything, a yellow slicker raincoat and rubber boots. Looking around.) Hmn. Very nice. Very nice.

MARK. Glad you like it.

BEVERLY. All the comforts of home. Amazing what you can do with a coffin if you put your mind to it.

MARK. *(Who would have found it difficult enough dealing with a postman, let alone this.)* What?!?

BEVERLY. Oh, sorry. Sorry. Introductions first. That way you'll know who you're throwing out. *(She extends her hand in a handshake.)* I'm Beverly. No doubt you've . . .

MARK. *(He doesn't shake hands.)* Yes.

BEVERLY. That's what I figured.

MARK. Brian's wife.

BEVERLY. Ex-wife.

MARK. Former.

BEVERLY. Yes. Former. Former wife. He prefers former, doesn't he?

MARK. *(Shakes her hand.)* Yes. I figured it was you.

BEVERLY. You did?

MARK. Yes . . . it wasn't hard.

BEVERLY. No, I guess not. *(She smiles.)* And you're . . . uh . . .

MARK. Yes.

BEVERLY. Yes. I figured.

MARK. Mark.

BEVERLY. Great. Well—

MARK. Well. (*Pause.*)

BEVERLY. Well, now that we know who we are . . . how about a drink.

MARK. A what?

BEVERLY. A drink. A drink.

MARK. Oh, no.

BEVERLY. No?

MARK. No. We don't keep any liquor here. I could get you some coffee or some penicillin, if you'd like.

BEVERLY. No. No. *I* was inviting *you*. (*Out of her tote bag she pulls a half finished bottle of Scotch.*) I had an accident with the Scotch on the way out here. There's quite a dent in it. (*She laughs*—MARK *doesn't.*) Anyway, we both look like we could use a little. Hmn?

MARK. No. I don't drink.

BEVERLY. (*Rummaging in her bag.*) Ah, a dope man.

MARK. Neither. I like to avoid as much poison as possible.

BEVERLY. I see.

MARK. Anyway, it's really not the time or place, is it?

BEVERLY. Oh, I don't know.

MARK. Well, you go ahead. If you feel you have to.

BEVERLY. No. No, really. I don't *need* it. I mean, I'm not . . . forget it. (*She looks remorsefully at the bottle, takes off the cap, takes a swig, replaces the cap and puts the bottle back in the tote bag.* MARK *stares at her, obviously displeased by the action. There is a pause.* BEVERLY *smiles.* MARK *does not.*) So. How is he?

MARK. Dying. How are you?

BEVERLY. (*Taken aback.*) Ooooops. Let's start again. Is he feeling any pain?

MARK. Are you?

BEVERLY. Strike two. Well, I think we've got it all

straight now. He's dying. I'm drunk. And you're pissed off. Did I leave anything out?

MARK. No, I think that just about covers it.

BEVERLY. Tell me. How is he?

MARK. Hard to say. One day he's flat on his ass, the next day he's running around like a two year old. But he is terminal—officially. They moved him down to these cottages because there's nothing they can do for him in the hospital. But he can't go home, either. There's some pain. But it's tolerable. At least he makes it seem tolerable. They keep shooting him full of cortisone.

BEVERLY. Ouch!

MARK. Yes. Ouch. You should be prepared, I guess.

BEVERLY. Prepared for what?

MARK. The cortisone.

BEVERLY. Why? They don't give it to the visitors, do they?

MARK. No. I mean it has side effects. It . . . well, you may not notice it, but the skin goes sort of white and puffy. It changed the shape of his face for a while, and he started to get really fat.

BEVERLY. His whole body?

MARK. Yes. His whole body.

BEVERLY. Charming.

MARK. Well, don't get too upset. A lot of it's been corrected, but he's still very pale. And he has fainting spells. They're harmless. Well, that's what they tell me. But it's embarrassing for him because he falls down a lot and his face gets a little purple for a minute.

BEVERLY. All the details. You're very graphic.

MARK. It happens a lot. The details aren't easy to forget.

BEVERLY. I guess not.

MARK. I just want you to know. If you're staying around. I mean, I think it would hurt him if people noticed.

BEVERLY. Well, if he turns purple and falls on the floor, it'd be sort of difficult not to notice, wouldn't it?

MARK. (*Taken aback.*) What?

BEVERLY. I mean, what do people *usually* do when it happens?

MARK. I don't know. I mean, there hasn't been anyone here except me and . . .

BEVERLY. And you have everything pretty much under control.

MARK. I do my best.

BEVERLY. I'm sure you do.

MARK. Look. I don't mean to be rude or stupid about this . . .

BEVERLY. Why not? I like people to be rude and stupid. It's one of the ways you can be sure they're still alive. Oh dear, I did it again, didn't I?

MARK. Yes. You have to understand—I mean, you will be careful, won't you?

BEVERLY. About what?

MARK. That's exactly what I mean. You're . . . I'm sorry, but you're very stoned, aren't you? And you're dressed in funny clothes, and you're saying a lot of funny things but I'm just not sure, frankly, what the fuck you're doing here.

BEVERLY. (*Still flip.*) Neither am I. You sure you wouldn't like a drink?

MARK. Positive. Look, please, don't you think it'd be better if you came back some other time, like tomorrow or next year or something?

BEVERLY. I'd just have to get drunk all over again.

MARK. I mean, it's sort of a delicate situation, right

now. He's had a very bad time of it and any kind of, well, disturbance . . .

BEVERLY. Such as me? Oh, you'll get used to it. You just have to think of me as your average tramp.

MARK. . . . any disturbance might be dangerous, especially psychologically and . . . Shit! I sound like an idiot, the way I'm talking. But you don't seem to be understanding a goddamn word I'm saying!

BEVERLY. No. I am. I am. You know, you don't *look* like a faggot.

MARK. Oh, for Christ's sake!

BEVERLY. No, I mean it . . . I mean, I didn't expect . . .

MARK. Well, you'll get used to it. You just have to think of me as your average cocksucker. All right?

BEVERLY. Good. Now we're getting someplace. Are you sure you wouldn't like a drink?

MARK. *No!* I would not like a drink. *You* have a drink. Have two. Take off your clothes. Make yourself at home. (*He grabs his jacket and heads for the door.*) When you're ready to throw up, the bathroom is in there. (*He exits.*)

BEVERLY. (*Left with the bottle.*) Hey!

(*The lights come up on the porch area where* STEVE *is just coming out of the cottage to join* MAGGIE *and* JOE.)

STEVE. Hey! Is this place bugged or what?

JOE. Bugged?

MAGGIE. (*Reaching into a shopping bag.*) I brought some Lysol. Here.

STEVE. No. Bugged. *Wired.* What do they do? Listen in with hidden cameras?

JOE. (*Laughing.*) Yeah. Every move. Every word.

MAGGIE. Joe, cut it out.

STEVE. (*Continuing.*) But they got wires near the bed.

JOE. That's for me. Don't worry about it.

MAGGIE. (*Changing the subject.*) Here. (*To* STEVE.) You take this stuff inside. And keep the noise down.

JOE. (*To* MAGGIE.) Come on in, Maggie. I'll show you around.

MAGGIE. No. I want to stay outside. For a while, it's nice.

STEVE. (*Runs back into the cottage.*) I'll get my guitar . . .

JOE. You like it, don't you?

MAGGIE. Sure. It's nice. (*Calling.*) Stephen, you help me with this . . .

JOE. (*Overlapping.*) I knew you would. I'll take you for a walk later. They got a swimming pool. And a tennis court. There's a little river, just a little one, runs back through the trees. Over there. I'll show you later. We got time. There's no hurry.

MAGGIE. Stephen!

JOE. Ah, leave him be. I'll get this. (*He starts to pick up the bags.*)

MAGGIE. No, you rest. Stephen!

JOE. I can get it. The more exercise I get, the better I feel.

MAGGIE. (*Stopping him.*) There's no sense pushing it, huh? Steve can do it. (STEVE *comes out of the cottage with his guitar. He sits down and starts to play it.*) Stephen! Put that thing down and give your father a hand.

JOE. (*To* STEVE.) Wait till you see, dad. From the north side, near the gate when you come in, you can

see the whole valley. All squared off and patched up
with farms like a quilt. Hundreds of them. I'll show
you.

STEVE. Farms? They got farms?

JOE. Yeah. Hundreds of them. Christ it was great
to get out of that city.

MAGGIE. Stephen, take this bag inside. Put this one
in the kitchen. (*To* JOE.) You got a kitchen?

JOE. Sure. A kitchen, a bathroom, two bedrooms, a
living room . . .

STEVE. (*Overlapping.*) We never did get our farm.
We should do that. We should get that farm. (*He takes
bag inside.*)

JOE. Well, maybe we should have.

MAGGIE. (*To* STEVE.) There's more here, when you're
finished, so hurry up.

JOE. A little place like this.

MAGGIE. Don't start on the farm, for God's sake. It
always ends up bad when you start on the farm.

STEVE. (*Returning.*) We could sit out every night,
singing and howling at the moon. (*He howls like a
wolf.*)

MAGGIE. (*Getting more and more agitated.*) Stephen,
be quiet. Where do you think you are? This goes in
the bedroom.

STEVE. Aren't you ever coming in?

MAGGIE. (*A little too firmly.*) I'll go in when I'm
good and ready. (STEVE *exits with suitcase.*)

JOE. (*Noticing* MAGGIE's *nervousness, trying to keep
things happy.*) It might have worked, Maggie. See
me all dressed up in coveralls, early morning, up with
the sun. What do you think?

MAGGIE. (*More irritated.*) It's a lot of work. I don't
want to hear about it.

JOE. A little hard work'll never kill you.

MAGGIE. Don't tell me about hard work.

JOE. It's good for you.

MAGGIE. Good for *you*. Not for me. Milk the cows, clean the chicken coop, who would have done that, huh?

STEVE. (*Returning.*) We could have had a couple hundred acres . . .

JOE. No, someplace small, something we could keep our hands on. Al and Lena had that place, we used to go every Sunday.

MAGGIE. It was dirty.

STEVE. No, it wasn't.

MAGGIE. And I never had anything to say to them, anyway. Out there in the sticks. Who do you see out there? Chickens and pigs.

JOE. They had neighbors.

MAGGIE. Chickens and pigs.

JOE. You get used to all that . . .

MAGGIE. I don't want to hear about it. Here, Stephen. It's the last one. Put it anywhere.

STEVE. (*To* MAGGIE.) You would too have liked it. Get a little chicken shit between your toes, kiss a few pigs . . . It'd change your whole disposition . . . (*He grabs the bag and* MAGGIE *and starts whirling her around.*)

MAGGIE. (*Almost laughing.*) Cut it out! Stephen!

STEVE. (*Starts to tickle her and push her toward the cottage.*) Come on inside, Chicken Lady. I'll show you the roost! (MAGGIE *is laughing hard now.* STEVE *clucks like a chicken, tickling her, and steering her toward the cottage.* JOE *laughs and joins them.*)

JOE. Come on, Maggie. We got you. (*He pushes her toward the cottage.*)

MAGGIE. (*Laughing hysterically.*) Joe . . . ! No
. . . I don't . . . !

STEVE. Chickens and pigs! Chickens and pigs!

JOE. Come on inside, Maggie. Come on!

MAGGIE. No . . . I don't . . . want to go inside
. . . No . . . ! Joe! (*Suddenly* MAGGIE *turns and
slaps* STEVE *hard across the face. She is terrified.*) I'm
not going in there! Now stop it! (*Nobody moves for
a moment.* STEVE *is stunned.* MAGGIE *turns away from
them.* JOE *goes to* STEVE *and puts his arm around him.*)

STEVE. I'm going inside to practice . . .

JOE. Sure.

STEVE. (*Picks up his guitar and goes to the cottage
door. Then he turns, looks at* MAGGIE. *Then he says
to* JOE . . .) There's a . . . there's a whole lot of shit
I got to tell you. We can talk, huh? Not to worry you,
but just so you know . . . There's a whole lot . . .
we can talk, huh?

JOE. (*Hugs* STEVE.) Sure, dad. (STEVE *goes inside.*
JOE *looks at* MAGGIE, *not knowing what came over
her.*) Maggie?

MAGGIE. I didn't tell him.

JOE. What?

MAGGIE. (*Still turned away from him.*) I didn't tell
him. Stephen. I didn't . . .

JOE. Oh, no. No, Maggie. What's the matter with
you?

MAGGIE. I couldn't.

JOE. He doesn't know? (MAGGIE *shakes her head
"No".*) What does he think? He thinks I'm going
home with you? Maggie? Why didn't you tell him?

MAGGIE. I couldn't.

JOE. Why not?

MAGGIE. Because . . . it isn't true. It isn't true. It isn't . . .

(*She runs off away from the cottage.* JOE *is stunned. He sits down on the porch steps and puts his head in his hands. The lights come up on the Interview Area.* AGNES *is pushing* FELICITY *to the area.* FELICITY *is wide awake now. She is about sixty or seventy years old. She is singing vaguely to herself. The* INTERVIEWER *is trying to get her attention with little success.*)

VOICE OF INTERVIEWER. . . . but you don't have to talk to us if you don't want to . . . Felicity? (*She continues to sing to herself.*) If you'd rather not talk now, we can wait until tomorrow. (*She pays no attention to him.*) Shall we do that? Shall we wait until tomorrow? (*No response.*) Felicity? (*No response.*) Well, why don't we do that, then? Why don't we wait, and later if you feel . . .

FELICITY. Piss poor.

VOICE OF INTERVIEWER. What?

FELICITY. Piss poor. Your attitude. It's a piss poor way to treat people.

VOICE OF INTERVIEWER. But, Felicity . . . (AGNES *returns to the kitchen area of the cottage.*)

FELICITY. But, but, but!

VOICE OF INTERVIEWER. Please . . .

FELICITY. Please what?! Alright. Alright. You want to talk? Let's talk. "I feel fine." Is that what you want to hear? Of course it is. I feel fine, there's no pain, I'm as blind as I was yesterday, my bowels are working—and that's all I got to say about it.

VOICE OF INTERVIEWER. We're only trying to help.

FELICITY. Well I appreciate your concern but I don't need any more help from you. Do I?

VOICE OF INTERVIEWER. Well, we don't know.

FELICITY. Of course you know. I've just told you. I've just said it, haven't I?

VOICE OF INTERVIEWER. Yes.

FELICITY. Well, then . . . there you are. There's nothing more to say. You should learn to listen.

VOICE OF INTERVIEWER. Yes.

FELICITY. What, have you got your friends out there again? All come to look at the dead people.

VOICE OF INTERVIEWER. Felicity . . .

FELICITY. He doesn't like me to say things like that. He's sensitive. Why don't you go hide yourself out there with the rest of them?

VOICE OF INTERVIEWER. Would you like me to . . . ?

FELICITY. No. (*Beat.*) No. You stay where you are.

VOICE OF INTERVIEWER. All right.

FELICITY. How do I look today?

VOICE OF INTERVIEWER. You look fine.

FELICITY. You're a liar. I look like I feel. I smell, too. (*She turns away from him.*)

VOICE OF INTERVIEWER. Are you tired, Felicity?

FELICITY. No.

VOICE OF INTERVIEWER. Do you want to talk some more today?

FELICITY. No.

VOICE OF INTERVIEWER. All right then. Do you want to go back to the cottage?

FELICITY. No.

VOICE OF INTERVIEWER. Will you tell us if you're in pain?

FELICITY. No.

VOICE OF INTERVIEWER. You could help us if you talked to us.

FELICITY. Help you? Help you? Don't make me laugh, I'll split a stitch. Which one of us is kicking the bucket? Me? Me or you?

VOICE OF INTERVIEWER. Well . . .

FELICITY. Come on. Spit it out. Don't be shy. You're not stupid on top of everything else, are you? One of us is dying and it isn't you, is it?

VOICE OF INTERVIEWER. No. You are the patient.

FELICITY. Patient?! Patient, hell! I'm the corpse. I have one lung, one plastic bag for a stomach, and two springs and a battery where my heart used to be. You cut me up and took everything that wasn't nailed down. Sons of bitches.

VOICE OF INTERVIEWER. But we're not your doctors, Mrs. Thomas.

FELICITY. (*Overlapping.*) We're not your doctors . . . Claire . . .

VOICE OF INTERVIEWER. What?

FELICITY. Claire . . .

VOICE OF INTERVIEWER. Mrs. Thomas? Are you alright?

FELICITY. I'm alright! I'm alright! I'll tell you when I'm not alright. It isn't five, is it? Is it five yet?

VOICE OF INTERVIEWER. Five?

FELICITY. Sons of bitches . . . my daughter, Claire.

VOICE OF INTERVIEWER. Yes.

FELICITY. She writes to me regularly. A letter almost every day. I have them at the cottage.

VOICE OF INTERVIEWER. That's very nice.

FELICITY. Yes!

VOICE OF INTERVIEWER. Where does she live?

FELICITY. Who?

VOICE OF INTERVIEWER. Your daughter, Claire.

FELICITY. Yes. I've kept them all—every letter she ever sent me.

VOICE OF INTERVIEWER. That's a good idea.

FELICITY. So I'll have them when I go home. She's a good girl, my Claire.

VOICE OF INTERVIEWER. Where is she now?

FELICITY. Now?

VOICE OF INTERVIEWER: Yes.

FELICITY. She's with me.

VOICE OF INTERVIEWER. Where?

FELICITY. Here. At the house.

VOICE OF INTERVIEWER. The house?

FELICITY. Yes. You don't run a place like this on dreams. It takes hard work. The property isn't much but the stock is good. We showed a clear profit in '63. Nobody was more surprised than I was—but we did it. How do I look today?

VOICE OF INTERVIEWER. You look fine. Do you want to talk about Claire?

FELICITY. I look terrible.

VOICE OF INTERVIEWER. The more we know, the easier it is for us to understand how you feel.

FELICITY. No! Claire isn't with me anymore. She'll be here soon. But she isn't here now. Agnes is with me now . . . (*She calls out.*) Agnes! (*To the* INTERVIEWER.) Agnes is my oldest.

VOICE OF INTERVIEWER. Yes, we . . .

FELICITY. (*Calling again.*) Agnes!!! (*The lights come up on the cottage behind* FELICITY. AGNES *is discovered inside, writing at a table. When she hears her Mother's voice, she gets up slowly, folds the paper she has been writing on, puts it into an envelope, seals the envelope and puts it into her pocket.* AGNES *is a very plain look-*

ing middle-aged woman—very neat, very tense, very tired. Hair drawn back tightly. She has tried all her life to do the right thing, and the attempt has left her very confused, awkward, and unsure of herself. When she hears her Mother call, she obediently goes to her.) Agnes!

VOICE OF INTERVIEWER. Mrs. Thomas . . . ?

FELICITY. *(Her voice and manner growing harder again.)* Claire has two children, now. Two beautiful, twin angels . . . *(Calling.)* Agnes! *(To* INTERVIEWER.*)* Agnes has me.

AGNES. *(Approaching the Interview Area.)* Yes, mama. I'm coming.

FELICITY. She's a little slow. It's not her fault. She takes after her father. Not too pretty, not too bright. Is she here yet?

AGNES. *(Standing behind* FELICITY'S *wheelchair.)* Yes, mama. I'm here.

FELICITY. *(To* INTERVIEWER.*)* There. You see what I mean? You be careful of Agnes. She's jealous.

AGNES. *(A little embarrassed.)* Mama . . . please.

FELICITY. Get me out of here.

AGNES. *(To* INTERVIEWER.*)* Is that all for today?

VOICE OF INTERVIEWER. Yes, thank you, Agnes, that's . . .

FELICITY. *(Overlapping.)* That's all. That's all! Now take me back.

AGNES. Yes, mama. *(She turns the wheelchair and starts to push it toward the cottage.)*

FELICITY. Easy! Easy! You'll upset my internal wire works.

AGNES. I'm sorry. *(Turning back to the* INTERVIEWER.*)* Same time tomorrow?

VOICE OF INTERVIEWER. Yes. And if you have time, Agnes, we'd like to talk to you.

AGNES. Me?

FELICITY. We'll see about tomorrow. You sons of bitches.

AGNES. (*To* INTERVIEWER.) All right.

FELICITY. Push, Agnes. Push!

AGNES. Yes, mama. Off we go. (*They go up to the kitchen area of the cottage.*)

FELICITY. That's the spirit. Put some balls into it!

(*Back in the cottage,* BRIAN *enters the living room area where* BEVERLY *is waiting.*)

BEVERLY. Caro! Caro! You old fart! Vieni qua!

BRIAN. (*Delighted.*) Sweet Jesus! Beverly!

BEVERLY. My God, he even remembers my name! What a mind! (*She hugs and kisses him.*)

BRIAN. What a picture!

BEVERLY. (*Taking off her coat to show her dress and jewels.*) All my medals. All of them! I wore as many of them as I could fit.

BRIAN. Fantastic.

BEVERLY. Everything I could carry. I tried to get X-rays done but there wasn't time. Inside and out. I'll strip later and show you all of it.

BRIAN. (*Laughing.*) Good. Good. What a surprise! (*Another embrace.*) I'm so happy you've come. Where's Mark? Have you met him?

BEVERLY. Oh, yes. He's beautiful. A little cool, but I'm sure there's a heart in there somewhere.

BRIAN. Where is he?

BEVERLY. Well . . . he's gone.

BRIAN. What?

BEVERLY. It's my fault. I made a very sloppy entrance. I think he left in lieu of punching me in the mouth.

BRIAN. I don't believe it.

BEVERLY. It's true. But I do like him.

BRIAN. Good. So do I.

BEVERLY. (*Insinuating.*) So I gather.

BRIAN. (*Cheerfully.*) Uh-uh. Careful.

BEVERLY. Is he any good?

BRIAN. Beverly!

BEVERLY. Well, what's it like?

BRIAN. 'It'?

BEVERLY. Yes. Him, you, it . . . you know I'm a glutton for pornography. Tell me, quick.

BRIAN. (*Laughs.*) Oh, no.

BEVERLY. No?

BRIAN. No. And that's final. I refuse to discuss it.

BEVERLY. Brian, that's not fair. Here I am all damp in my panties and you're changing the subject. Now come on. Tell me all about it.

BRIAN. Absolutely not. I'm much too happy.

BEVERLY. Brian . . . I was married to you. I deserve an explanation. Isn't that what I'm supposed to say?

BRIAN. Yes, but you're too late. No excuses, no explanations. (*Singing.*) He is my sunshine, my only sunshine . . . He's the—pardon the expression—cream in my coffee—the milk in my tea—He will always be my necessity . . .

BEVERLY. Ah, but is he enough?

BRIAN. More than enough.

BEVERLY. Shucks.

BRIAN. (*Laughs.*) Sorry, but it's out of my hands. All of it. Some supreme logic has taken hold of my life. And in the absence of any refutable tomorrow, every insane thing I do today seems to make a great deal of sense.

BEVERLY. What the hell does that mean?

BRIAN. It means there are more important things in this world.

BEVERLY. More important than what?

BRIAN. More important than worrying about who is fucking whom.

BEVERLY. You *are* happy, aren't you?

BRIAN. Ecstatic. I'm even writing again.

BEVERLY. Oh, my God. You couldn't be *that* happy!

BRIAN. Why not?

BEVERLY. Brian, you're a terrible writer, and you know it.

BRIAN. So?

BEVERLY. Outside of that wonderful book of crossword puzzles, your greatest contribution to the literary world was your retirement.

BRIAN. (*Finishes the sentence with her.*) . . . was my retirement. Yes. Well, the literary world, such as it is, will have to brave the storm. Because I'm back.

BEVERLY. But why?

BRIAN. Pure and unadulterated masochism. No. It's just that when they told me I was on the way out . . . so to speak . . . I realized that there was a lot to do that I hadn't done yet. So I figured I better get off my ass and start working.

BEVERLY. Doing what?

BRIAN. Everything! Everything! It's amazing what you can accomplish. Two rotten novels, twenty-seven boring stories, several volumes of tortured verse—including twelve Italian sonnets and one epic investigation of the Firth of Forth Bridge . . .

BEVERLY. The what?

BRIAN. The bridge. The railroad bridge in Scotland. The one Hitchcock used in 'The Thirty-Nine Steps.' You remember. We saw the picture on our honeymoon.

BEVERLY. Oh, yes.

BRIAN. And I swore that one day I would do a poem about it. Well, I've done it.

BEVERLY. Thank God.

BRIAN. Yes. Four hundred stanzas—trochaic hexameters with rhymed couplets. (*He demonstrates the rhythm.*) *Da*-da-da, *Da*-da-da, *Da*-da-da, *Da*-da-da, *Da*-da-da, *Da*-da-da, *Da*-da-da-*Dee!* It's perfectly ghastly. But it's done. I've also completed nearly one hundred and thirty-six epitaphs, the largest contribution to the Forest Lawn catalogue since Edna St. Vincent Millay, and I've also done four autobiographies.

BEVERLY. Four?!

BRIAN. Yes. Each one under a different name. There's a huge market for dying people right now. My agent assured me.

BEVERLY. I don't believe it.

BRIAN. It's true. And then we thought we'd give them each one of those insipid dirty titles—like 'Sex . . . And the Dying Man'!

BEVERLY. Or 'The Sensuous Corpse.'

BRIAN. Very good.

BEVERLY. (*Affectionately.*) You idiot. What else?

BRIAN. Not too much. For a while they were giving me this drug and my vision was doubled. I couldn't really see to write. So I started to paint.

BEVERLY. Paint?

BRIAN. Pictures. I did fourteen of them. Really extraordinary stuff. I was amazed. I mean, you know

I can't draw a straight line. But with my vision all cockeyed—I could do a bowl of fruit that sent people screaming from the room.

BEVERLY. I can believe it. So now you're painting.

BRIAN. No, no. They changed the medication. Now all the fruit just looks like fruit again. But I did learn to drive.

BEVERLY. A car?

BRIAN. Yes.

BEVERLY. Good grief.

BRIAN. Not very well, but with a certain style and sufficient accuracy to keep myself alive—although that is beside the point, isn't it? Let's see, what else? I've become a master at chess, bridge, poker, and mah-jongg, I finally bought a television set, I sold the house and everything that was in it, closed all bank accounts, got rid of all stocks, bonds, securities, everything.

BEVERLY. What did you do with the money?

BRIAN. I put it in a sock and buried it on Staten Island.

BEVERLY. You did, didn't you?

BRIAN. Almost. I gave back my American Express card, my BankAmericard—severed *all* my patriotic connections. I even closed my account at Bloomingdale's.

BEVERLY. This is serious.

BRIAN. You're damn right it is. I sleep only three hours a day, I never miss a dawn or a sunset, I say and do everything that comes into my head. I even sent letters to everyone I know and told them exactly what I think of them . . . just so none of the wrong people show up for the funeral. And finally . . . I went to Passaic, New Jersey.

BEVERLY. For God's sake, why?!

BRIAN. Because I had no desire to go there.

BEVERLY. Then why did you go?

BRIAN. Because I wanted to be absolutely *sure* I had no desire to go there.

BEVERLY. And now you know.

BRIAN. Yes. I spent two weeks at a Holiday Inn and had all my meals at Howard Johnson.

BEVERLY. Jesus! You've really gone the limit.

BRIAN. Believe me, Passaic is beyond the limit. Anyway, that's what I've been doing. Every day in every way, I get smaller and smaller. There's practically nothing left of me.

BEVERLY. You're disappearing before my very eyes.

BRIAN. Good. You see, the only way to beat this thing is to leave absolutely nothing behind. I don't want to leave anything unsaid, undone . . . not a word, not even a lonely, obscure, silly, worthless thought. I want it all used up. All of it. That's not too much to ask, is it?

BEVERLY. No.

BRIAN. That's what I thought. Then I can happily leap into my coffin and call it a day. Lie down, close my eyes, shut my mouth and disappear into eternity.

BEVERLY. As easy as that?

BRIAN. Like falling off a log. (BRIAN *laughs.* BEVERLY *laughs.. And then the laughter slowly dies.* BEVERLY *goes to him, takes his hands, holds them for a moment, Long Pause.*) It shows. Doesn't it?

BEVERLY. You're shaking.

BRIAN. I can't help it. I'm scared to death.

BEVERLY. It's a lot to deal with.

BRIAN. No. Not really. It's a little thing. I mean, all this . . . this is easy. Pain, discomfort . . . that's all part of living. And I'm just as alive now as I ever was. And I *will* be alive right up to the last moment. *That's* the hard part, that last fraction of a second—when you know that the next fraction of a second—I can't seem to fit that moment into my life . . . You're absolutely alone facing an absolute unknown and there is absolutely nothing you can do about it . . . except give in. (*Pause.*)

BEVERLY. That's how I felt the first time I lost my virginity.

BRIAN. (*Laughs.*) How was it the second time?

BEVERLY. Much easier.

BRIAN. There. You see? The real trouble with dying is you only get to do it once. (BRIAN *drifts into the thought.*)

BEVERLY. (*Pulling him back.*) I brought you some champagne.

BRIAN. I'm sorry. I must be the most tedious person alive.

BEVERLY. As a matter of fact, you are. Thank God you won't be around much longer.

BRIAN. (*Looking at the champagne.*) I hope you don't think I'm going to pass away drunk. I intend to be cold sober.

BEVERLY. No. No. I thought we could break it on your ass and shove you off with a great bon voyage, confetti and streamers all over the grave.

BRIAN. (*Laughing.*) Perfect. Perfect. I've missed your foolishness.

BEVERLY. You hated my foolishness.

BRIAN. I never understood it.

BEVERLY. Neither did I. But it was the only way. The only way I knew.

BRIAN. Well, all these roads, they all go to Rome, as they say.

BEVERLY. Yes. But why is it I always seem to end up in Naples?

(BRIAN *and* BEVERLY *embrace. The lights come up on the kitchen area of the cottage where* AGNES *is singing quietly to* FELICITY.)

AGNES. (*Singing.*)
Holy God, we praise thy name
Lord of all, we bow before Thee
And on earth thy scepter claim
All in heaven above adore Thee.

FELICITY. (*Who appeared to be asleep.*) What the hell is that?

AGNES. It's a hymn, mama.

FELICITY. Hymn! The time for hymns is when I'm in the coffin. Sing us a song!

AGNES. A song?

FELICITY. You know what a song is, don't you?

AGNES. Of course I know what a song is, but I don't think I know anything . . .

FELICITY. (*Singing.*)
'Roll me over, in the clover,
Lay me down, roll me over, do it again . . .'

AGNES. Mama, people can hear you.

FELICITY.
Do them good.
'This is number one and the fun is just begun
Lay me down, roll me over, do it again . . .'

AGNES. All right, mama. I'll get you some tea.

FELICITY. (*Ignoring her.*)
'Roll me over, in the clover
Lay me down, roll me over, do it again . . .'

AGNES. Would you like that? Would you like some tea, mama?

FELICITY. Put me by the table.

FELICITY. (*More singing.*)
'This is number two and his hand is on my shoe. Lay me down, roll me over, do it again . . .'

AGNES. You should try to rest, mama. This medicine does no good if you exhaust yourself . . .

(AGNES *wheels her to the table.*)

FELICITY. Other side! Other side! (AGNES *moves her to the other side of the table.*)

FELICITY.
'This is number three and his hand is on my knee. Lay me down, roll me over . . .'' (FELICITY *feels for the edge of the table.*)
Closer! Closer!

AGNES. We've done enough singing, now, mama. I want you to stop. Please.

AGNES. (*Pushing her closer to the table.*) There. Is that all right?

FELICITY. (*Ignoring her.*) 'This is number four and . . .' I don't remember four. What's four?

AGNES. (*Setting up a game of checkers.*) I don't know, mama. I don't think I know this song.

FELICITY. 'This is number five and his hand is on my thigh . . .' Do you know that one?

AGNES. No, mama. I don't.

FELICITY. They'll pass you by, Agnes. They will.

AGNES. Who, mama?

FELICITY. They'll leave you at the station with your suitcase in your hand and a big gardenia tacked onto your collar. Sons of bitches.

AGNES. I'm not anxious to be going anywhere.

FELICITY. 'This is number six and his hands are on my tits . . .'

AGNES. Mama!

FELICITY. Does *that* make you anxious?

AGNES. No.

FELICITY. Well, it makes *me* anxious. And I haven't even *got* tits anymore.

AGNES. I'll get you some tea, mama.

FELICITY. Tea . . . tea . . . tea . . . !

AGNES. Please, mama. I'm very tired.

FELICITY. (*At the top of her lungs.*) 'This is number seven and we're on our way to heaven. . .'!

AGNES. (*Suddenly and violently screams at her.*) Mama!!!! *Stop it!!*

(FELICITY *stops singing. She looks hurt, confused. She seems to drift off again as she did earlier, all her energy draining away.* AGNES *covers her mouth quickly, immediately ashamed and sorry for her outburst. There is a long silence.* BRIAN *goes to the Stage Left porch.* JOE *crosses to the Downstage porch and sits on the camp stool.*)

FELICITY. (*Very gentle, very weak.*) Put 'em away. Put 'em away. Shoot 'em and bury them. You can't get good milk from sick cows. Can you?

AGNES. No, mama. You can't.

FELICITY. They're not doing anybody any good. Standing around, making noises like it mattered. Bursting their bellies and there's nothing good inside. Just a lot of bad milk. Put 'em away. You see to that machinery.

AGNES. Yes, mama. I will.

FELICITY. It wants attention.

AGNES. We'll manage. We can sell off some of the land, if we have to.

FELICITY. But not the house.

AGNES. No, not the house. We'll keep the house.

FELICITY. What . . . what time did you say it was?

AGNES. Oh . . . about four. Four-fifteen . . .

FELICITY. Claire? Claire . . . ?

AGNES. No, mama. It's Agnes.

FELICITY. It hurts . . . hurts now . . .

AGNES. I know, mama . . .

FELICITY. Make it stop. Make it stop now . . .

AGNES. I'll give you some of the medicine.

FELICITY. Yes. With some tea. Could I have it with some tea?

AGNES. Yes, mama. I think so.

FELICITY. Just one cup. Very weak.

AGNES. Yes, mama. I'll make it for you. (*She lets go of* FELICITY'S *hand and goes to make the tea.*)

FELICITY. (*A sudden small panic.*) Agnes . . . !? (*She reaches out for* AGNES, *searching the air for her hand.*)

AGNES. Here, mama, here. I'm just going to make the tea.

FELICITY. Yes. All right. (*She panics again.*) Agnes!

AGNES. (*Takes wet cloth and wrings it out.*) Yes, mama. I'm here. (*She goes to* FELICITY *and wipes her brow with the cloth.*) It's all right. I'll get you your tea and then I'll read you your letter.

(STEVE *starts to play "Goodnight Irene" on his guitar.*
    MARK *crosses to the Down Right Interview Area.*)

FELICITY. Where are they now?

AGNES. Let me check the calendar.

MARK. I don't want to talk about it. It doesn't do any good to talk about it. I mean, it's just words. Isn't it? Little mirrors. You keep hanging them up like they mean something. You put labels on them. This one is true. This one is false. This one is broken . . . You can see right through it. Well, it all depends on how you look at it. *Doesn't* it? (MAGGIE *enters.*)

FELICITY. When did they say they were coming?

AGNES. Let's see. Today is the fifth. The fifth of May.

MAGGIE. I called home. I told them we got here all right. I told them . . . I don't know . . . I wanted to talk to pop. But he was asleep. He takes naps now. He gets up every morning at seven and he goes to church. All his life—since the day he was married—you couldn't get him near a church. Now he's seventy-five and he's there every morning. I asked him why, he said it was between him and God. What does that mean?

FELICITY. When did they say they were coming?

AGNES. Yes. Mexico. They should be passing right through the center of Mexico today.

FELICITY. They're moving awfully slow, don't you think?

AGNES. Well, it's difficult for them, I imagine. Trying to get so much organized, a family, a whole family and everything else . . . You can't just drop everything and leave. Especially if you live in a foreign country, as they do . . .

BRIAN. I asked one of the doctors. I said, why do I shake like this? He said he didn't know . . . I said, well . . . is it a symptom or is it because of the drugs? He said, no. And I said, well, why then? I don't seem to have any control of it. I'm feeling perfectly all right and then I shake. And he said, try to think if it's ever happened before . . . that kind of thing. And I couldn't. For a long time. And then I remembered being very young . . . I was—oh—five years old. My father was taking me to Coney Island. And we got separated on the train. And I kept trying to ask for directions but I couldn't talk because I was shaking so badly. It was because I was frightened. That's . . . uh . . . That's why I shake now . . . Isn't it?

FELICITY. (*In great pain.*) Agnes . . . !!! Agnes.

AGNES. Yes, mama, here. It's all right.

FELICITY. Agnes! Sons of bitches . . .

AGNES. It's all right. It's all right.

JOE. I get dreams now. Every night. I get dreams so big. I never used to dream. But now, every night, so big. Every person I ever knew in my life coming through my room, talking and talking and sometimes singing and dancing. Jumping all around my bed. And I get up to go with them, but I can't. The sheets are too heavy and I can't move to save my life. And they keep talking and calling my name, whispering so loud it hurts my ears . . . 'Joe' and 'Joe' and laughing and singing and I know every one of them and they pull at my arms and my legs and I still can't move. And I'm laughing and singing, too, inside, where you can't hear it. And it hurts so bad, but I can't feel it. And I yell back at them, every person I ever knew, and they don't hear me, either, and then the room gets brighter and brighter. So bright I can't see anything anymore. Nobody. Not even me. It's all gone. All white. All gone.

FELICITY. Agnes . . . !!

AGNES. Yes, mama.

FELICITY. When did they say they were coming?

AGNES. I don't know, mama. Soon. Soon.

FELICITY. As long as we know . . . As long as we know they're coming.

AGNES. Well, of course they're coming. You wait and see . . . One afternoon, we'll be sitting here, having tea, and that door will fly open like the gates of heaven and there they'll be . . . (*She takes a capsule from a small bottle and adds the medication to the cup of tea.*) two twin angels and our bright-eyed little girl. You wait and see, mama. You wait . . . (*She takes the cup to* FELICITY *and then notices that she is asleep.*) Mama? Oh, mama.

BRIAN. (*Going to* BEVERLY.) Dance with me, Bev.

BEVERLY. My pleasure, sir.

MAGGIE. Joe?

JOE. We got to tell him, Maggie. We got to tell him.

AGNES. Rest, mama . . . rest . . .

MARK. It'll all be over in a minute. It just seems to take forever. (*The lights fade out.*)

END OF ACT ONE

ACT TWO

Evening.

MUSIC is coming from the living room area . . . a recording of "Don't Sit Under The Apple Tree." BEVERLY is dancing around alone, BRIAN is sitting on the sofa watching her. MARK is in the kitchen area getting a glass of milk.

As the lights come up, however, we focus on the porch area where MAGGIE is seated, staring off at the sunset. JOE comes down to her, carrying a cup of coffee.

JOE. It's getting dark, Maggie.

MAGGIE. *(Very distant.)* It's pretty.

JOE. Yeah. *(Pause.)* You can't sit out here all night. Huh? *(MAGGIE doesn't answer.)* I brought you some coffee. *(MAGGIE takes it.)*

MAGGIE. I'm all right. I'm all right. I just need some time, that's all.

JOE. I'll get you a sweater.

(JOE goes back into the cottage, to the Upstage Center room and sits. Our focus shifts now into the living room area. It looks like a small party. BEVERLY is carrying on and BRIAN is enjoying every minute of it. MARK is not.)

BRIAN. Another drink for Beverly and then she can show us her scars.

51

BEVERLY. Medals, medals! Not scars.

BRIAN. Well, we won't argue the perspective.

MARK. (*Giving her a drink.*) I don't understand.

BEVERLY. Dancing contests. That's a euphemism for balling. First prize, second prize, third prize . . . sometimes just a citation for style. I like to keep Brian informed.

MARK. You lost me.

BEVERLY. Look. (*She takes off an earring.*) Peter somebody. Diamonds. Really. Very pure, very idealistic, an architect. Form follows function . . . I never understood it. (*She tosses the earring into her tote bag.*)

BRIAN. (*Toasting with his milk.*) To Peter!

BEVERLY. (*Drinks.*) One among many. (*She takes off a bracelet.*) This one's copper. A doctor in Colorado Springs. Said it would cure my arthritis and he'd take care of the rest. He didn't. (*She drops the bracelet on the sofa.*)

BRIAN. (*Toasting again.*) Colorado Springs!

BEVERLY. (*Drinks.*) Anyway, I didn't have arthritis. (*She points to a brooch.*) This one, God knows. A family heirloom and would I join the collection. No, thank you. (*Takes off a chain necklace with a tooth on it and swings it in a circle.*) Claus. Norwegian shark tooth or something. A thousand and one positions, and each one lasted several hours. I couldn't. (*She drops it.*)

BRIAN. I should hope not.

BEVERLY. But I tried. (*Takes another, very similar to the previous one, but smaller.*) Claus' brother. If at first you don't succeed . . . (*Points at a bracelet.*) A Russian in Paris. (*Another bracelet.*) A Frenchman in Moscow. (*Taking off an ankle bracelet.*) Ah . . . a

Tunisian in Newfoundland. Really. We met at an airport and made it between flights under his grass skirt. (*Drops it on the couch and then takes off two tiaras.*) Two lovely ladies in Biarritz.

BRIAN. Oh . . .

BEVERLY. No comment, thank you. (*Drops it on the sofa.*) Oh . . . yes. The Jean Jacques collection. (*Taking off several other pieces.*) Jean Jacques. Jean Jacques. Jean Jacques. Jean Jacques. Jean Jacques. You might say I took him for everything he was worth. You'd be wrong. There was a whole lot more I couldn't get my hands on. (*Toasting.*) A big one for Jean Jacques.

BRIAN. (*Toasting.*) Jean Jacques!

BEVERLY. (*A little dizzy.*) I'm getting sloppy. I tried. Dear Brian, how I tried. (*To* MARK.) You're the scholar. What's the exact declension of incompatibility? I tried, they tried, we tried . . .

MARK. That's not a declension. That's a conjugation.

BEVERLY. No, it wasn't. Not once. Not a single conjugator in the bunch. Not one real dancer. Not one real jump to the music, flat out, no count, foot stomping crazy-man . . . just a lot of tired "declining" people who really didn't want to do anything but sit the next one out. What else? Oh. Last and least, my favorite dress. A gap here, a stain there, a spilled drink, a catch, a tear . . . spots you can hardly see, that won't come out . . . people I hardly knew.

MARK. It looks walked over.

BEVERLY. Over and over again. Stitch it up, tie it up, wrap it up . . . it keeps coming back for more. Greedy little bitch. Here's a good one. A very well dressed man on a train. Put his hand here, on my leg, kept saying over and over again, 'Trust me, trust me,' and all the time he was beating off under his coat.

MARK. That's pathetic.

BEVERLY. Oh, I don't know. I think he liked me. Don't you think so? I mean the car was full of attractive younger women and the bastard chose me.

MARK. You must have been his type.

BRIAN. Mark!

MARK. I'm sorry. It just came out.

BEVERLY. That's all right.

MARK. It's not all right, it stinks.

BEVERLY. Okay. It stinks. Forget it. Here's to all of them. The young, the old, the black, the white, the yellow, the lame, the hale, the feebleminded, the poor, the rich, the small and the well endowed . . . all of them. Here's hoping there's better where *they* came from.

MARK. (*Getting his jacket and going towards the door.*) I'm going out for a walk.

BEVERLY. Oh, no. How are we ever going to get to know each other if you keep leaving the room?

BRIAN. Don't go, Mark.

MARK. I need some air. (*He starts to go.*)

BEVERLY. No. Stay. Come on. Please. (*She gets the champagne bottle.*)

MARK. Please what? You don't need me here, you've got a captive audience.

BEVERLY. Come on. We'll open the champagne and I'll shut up for a while.

MARK. Thanks, but I already told you . . .

BEVERLY. (*Forcing off the cork.*) It's good stuff. I only look cheap. Really. Are you sure you wouldn't like . . . (*The cork flies off and* BEVERLY *accidentally spills the contents of the bottle on* MARK.) a drink?

MARK. (*Sopping wet.*) No. Thank you.

BEVERLY. (*Really embarrassed, somewhere between*

giggling and crying.) Oh, God, I'm sorry. Talk about tedious people. I think I feel an exit coming up.

BRIAN. (*Goes to her, comforting.*) You look very beautiful, Beverly. I should have noticed when I walked in.

BEVERLY. I'm tired and drunk.

BRIAN. And beautiful.

BEVERLY. I'll miss you, you fucker.

BRIAN. I'll miss you, too.

BEVERLY. (*To* MARK.) Look what I've done. (*She starts to take the jacket from him.*)

MARK. (*Not letting go.*) It's all right.

BEVERLY. No. It's not. I've ruined it.

MARK. All right, you've ruined it.

BEVERLY. I'll send you another one.

MARK. No, I'll have it cleaned.

BEVERLY. It won't come out.

MARK. Please!

BRIAN. (*Grabbing the jacket and throwing it down.*) My God, it's only a jacket. Two sleeves, a collar, a piece of cloth. It was probably made by a machine in East Podunk. Why are we wasting this time?

MARK. Brian, take it easy . . .

BRIAN. No! Not easy. Not easy at all! At this very moment, twelve million stars are pumping light in and out of a three hundred and sixty degree notion of a limited universe. Not easy. At this very moment, a dozen Long Island oysters are stranded in some laboratory in Chicago, opening and closing to the rhythm of the tide—over a thousand miles away. Not easy. At this very moment, the sun is probably hurtling out of control, defying ninety percent of all organized religion —plummeting toward a massive world collision that was predicted simultaneously by three equally archaic cultures who had barely invented the wheel. At this very moment, some simple peasant in Mexico is planting seeds in his veins with the blind hope that flowers will bloom on his body before the frost kills him! And here we stand, the combined energy of our three magnificent minds focused irrevocably on a jacket. (*He puts the jacket on sofa to dry.*) My God. There are more important things I promise you. (MARK *does not respond.* BRIAN *goes to* BEVERLY *and takes her in his arms.*) Come on, my beauty, I'll show you a dancer. (*They begin to do the Lindy.* BRIAN *turns on the tape recorder and "Don't Sit Under the Apple Tree" starts to play.*)

BEVERLY. (*Laughing.*) Brian! Stop! (*Suddenly* BRIAN *falters. Breathless, he starts to fall, catches himself, and then falls.* BEVERLY *goes to him.*) Brian?! Are you all . . . ?

BRIAN. No! No. It's all right. I'm all right. He walks, he talks, he falls down, he gets up. Life goes on.

MARK. Let me give you a hand.

BRIAN. Leave me alone. (*Carefully he exits to the bedroom, but bumps into the end table on his way.* BEVERLY *looks anxiously at* MARK.)

BEVERLY. Do you think you should . . . ?

MARK. No. No.

(MARK *doesn't move. He seems frozen, terrified. He shakes his head "No" and turns away. Finally,* BEVERLY *follows* BRIAN *to the bedroom.* BEVERLY *exits.* MARK *picks up the bottle, turns off the recorder, sits down and starts drinking it from the bottle. At the same time,* AGNES *comes down to the stool at Down Right porch area, which becomes her Interview Area.*)

AGNES. (*Speaking to the* INTERVIEWER.) I shouldn't stay too long.

VOICE OF INTERVIEWER. (*At Down Left stool, but still miked.*) Yes. We won't keep you.

AGNES. You said you wanted to see me. Are there people there?

VOICE OF INTERVIEWER. Yes.

AGNES. I don't know what I can tell you.

VOICE OF INTERVIEWER. Well . . .

AGNES. The doctors saw her yesterday. They said they were going to change the medication, and after that, they weren't sure . . . Oh, but they must have told you all this.

VOICE OF INTERVIEWER. Yes.

AGNES. Oh. What . . . what was it you wanted to know, then.

VOICE OF INTERVIEWER. Well, we wanted to know about you.

AGNES. (*Almost smiles.*) Me? Oh, that's . . . (*Then worried.*) Why? I've done everything that . . . just like the nurse tells me. I've been very careful to . . .

VOICE OF INTERVIEWER. No. No. It isn't that. You're doing very well with her. Much better than anyone could ask. We know that.

AGNES. Then . . . what?

VOICE OF INTERVIEWER. Well, we were just wondering how you were?

AGNES. (*Relieved.*) Oh. I'm fine. Is that what you mean? I'm fine.

VOICE OF INTERVIEWER. Yes.

AGNES. I'm fine.

VOICE OF INTERVIEWER. Good.

AGNES. Yes. I'm a little tired. And sometimes a headache . . . I used to get headaches.

VOICE OF INTERVIEWER. Oh?

AGNES. Yes. Terrible headaches. Mama always said they were psychosomatic. She said if I concentrated hard enough, they would go away.

VOICE OF INTERVIEWER. And did they?

AGNES. As a matter of fact, they did. Not right away. But after a while . . .

VOICE OF INTERVIEWER. Do you still get them?

AGNES. What . . . ?

VOICE OF INTERVIEWER. The headaches. Do you still get them?

AGNES. I don't know. I used to get them so often. Now sometimes I don't know I have them—until they go away. You get used to them and you don't feel any different until they're gone. And I . . . what was it you wanted to ask me?

VOICE OF INTERVIEWER. Tell us about Claire.

AGNES. What?

VOICE OF INTERVIEWER. Claire. Felicity has been telling us that . . .

AGNES. Claire.

VOICE OF INTERVIEWER. Your sister.

AGNES. Oh, Claire . . .

VOICE OF INTERVIEWER. Yes.

AGNES. Claire is my sister.

VOICE OF INTERVIEWER. Yes.

AGNES. (*With great reluctance.*) We were very close. Our whole family. Especially after my father died. We were just children then. Mama worked very hard to keep us together. We had a dairy farm. It was a beautiful place. Big, old house . . . 1873. And so much land. It seemed even bigger then . . . I was so little. We were very happy. And then Claire . . . there was a boy . . . well, she left us . . . just like that. She was a lot like Mama. They would fight and yell and throw things at each other . . . they got along very well. Claire was so beautiful. I would hide in my room. I got so frightened when they fought, but . . . I don't know . . . suddenly the fight would be over and Mama would throw open her arms and curse the day she bore children and Claire would laugh and then Mama would laugh and hug her close . . . and then all of us, we would laugh . . . I can still hear us . . . But she left. And we never heard from her. Almost a year. The longest year I can remember. Mama waited and waited, but she never wrote or came back to visit . . . nothing. And then one morning, we received a phone call from a man in Louisiana. There was an accident . . . something. And Claire was dead. They said at first they thought she was going to be all right, but she was hemorrhaging and . . . This is very hard to remember.

VOICE OF INTERVIEWER. But these letters from Claire.

AGNES. Yes. You see, it was after Claire died that Mama started to get sick. All of a sudden, she was 'old.' And she isn't, you know. But she just seemed to give up. I couldn't bring her out of it. Claire could have. But I couldn't. We lost the farm, the house, everything. One thing led to another. The letters . . . uh . . . It was after one of the last operations. Mama came home from the hospital and she seemed very happy. She was much stronger than ever. She laughed and joked and made fun of me, just like she used to . . . and then she told me she had written a letter while she was in the hospital . . . to Claire . . . and she said she was very nice to her and she forgave her for not writing and keeping in touch and she asked her to come home to visit and to bring her children . . .

Claire had been dead for a long time then. I didn't know what to do. I tried to tell her . . . I tried . . . but she wouldn't listen . . . And, of course, no letter came. No reply. And Mama asked every day for the mail. Every day I had to tell her no, there wasn't any. Every day. I kept hoping she would forget, but she didn't. And when there wasn't any letter for a long time, she started to get worse. She wouldn't talk and when she did she accused me of being jealous and hiding the letters and sometimes . . . I didn't know what to do . . . So . . . (*Pause.*)

VOICE OF INTERVIEWER. How long have you been writing these letters?

AGNES. Almost two years . . . You're not angry with me, are you?

VOICE OF INTERVIEWER. No.

AGNES. It means so much to her. It's important to her. It's something to hope for. You have to have something. People *need* something to keep them going.

VOICE OF INTERVIEWER. Do they?

AGNES. Yes. Sometimes I think, if we can wait long enough, something will happen. Oh, not that Mama will get better, but something . . . So I write the letters. I don't mind. It's not difficult. I read little things in books and newspapers and I make up what's happening. Sometimes I just write whatever comes into my head. You see, Mama doesn't really listen to them anymore. She used to. It used to be the only time I could talk to her. But now it doesn't matter what they say. It's just so she knows that Claire is coming.

VOICE OF INTERVIEWER. What happens when Claire doesn't show up?

AGNES. Oh, but I don't think that will happen. I, mean, Mama . . . well, she won't . . . I mean, even if . . .

VOICE OF INTERVIEWER. You mean she'll probably die before she even finds out.

AGNES. (*Nods her head.*) Yes.

VOICE OF INTERVIEWER. What will *you* do then, Agnes?

AGNES. (*Surprised by the question, she looks out at the* INTERVIEWER *for a long time. Then . . .*) It makes her happy.

VOICE OF INTERVIEWER. Does it?

AGNES. (*More confused.*) I don't know.

VOICE OF INTERVIEWER. What about you, Agnes?

AGNES. Me?

VOICE OF INTERVIEWER. Does it make you happy?

AGNES. Me?

VOICE OF INTERVIEWER. Yes.

AGNES. (*She touches her head lightly.*) Please, I . . . I should be getting back.

VOICE OF INTERVIEWER. Agnes?

AGNES. Sometimes she does things now, I don't know why . . . I . . . (*Trying to accuse the* INTERVIEWER.) The pain is much worse. This medicine you've given her . . . it doesn't help.

VOICE OF INTERVIEWER. Yes, we know. It may be necessary to move her up to the hospital again.

AGNES. But you said before . . .

VOICE OF INTERVIEWER. I know.

AGNES. And now?

VOICE OF INTERVIEWER. It's hard to say.

AGNES. No.

VOICE OF INTERVIEWER. I'm sorry.

AGNES. No, you're not sorry. You don't know anything about sorry. You put her in some room. You do one more operation. You wrap her up in your machines. You scribble on her chart. And then you go away. You don't know about sorry.

VOICE OF INTERVIEWER. We had thought that it wouldn't go on this long, but there's nothing we can do about it.

AGNES. *But I don't want it to go on.* You promised . . . it can't! Even when she's asleep now, she has dreams. I can tell. I hear them. You keep saying, a few days, a few days. But it's weeks and months . . . all winter and now the spring . . .

VOICE OF INTERVIEWER. She has a strong will.

AGNES. (*Almost laughs.*) Oh, yes. I know that.

VOICE OF INTERVIEWER. Sometimes that's enough to keep a very sick person alive for a long time.

AGNES. But why? Why? When it hurts so bad? Why does she want to keep going like this? Why?

VOICE OF INTERVIEWER. She's waiting for Claire.

AGNES. (*Stunned.*) What . . . ? What did you say?

VOICE OF INTERVIEWER. It's what we call 'making a bargain.' She's made up her mind that she's not going to die until Claire arrives.

AGNES. (*Denying it.*) Oh, no . . . no . . .

VOICE OF INTERVIEWER. . . . it might easily be the reason. Now that you've explained about the letters.

AGNES. . . . no . . . no . . .

VOICE OF INTERVIEWER. Agnes . . . ?

AGNES. . . . no . . . it isn't true . . . it isn't . . .

VOICE OF INTERVIEWER. Perhaps it isn't . . . (*In the cottage,* FELICITY *is slowly waking up. She mumbles.*)

FELICITY. . . . Claire . . .

AGNES. It isn't wrong to hope . . .

VOICE OF INTERVIEWER. Agnes . . . ?

AGNES. . . . waiting for . . .

FELICITY. . . . Claire . . .

AGNES. . . . no . . . she can't . . . she can't do that . . . she can't!!!

VOICE OF INTERVIEWER. Agnes . . .

AGNES. (*Rising.*) No. Please. I have to go . . . I have to go back . . .

VOICE OF INTERVIEWER. Listen to me . . .

AGNES. No! . . . I don't want to.

VOICE OF INTERVIEWER. Will you come back tomorrow?

AGNES. Tomorrow?

FELICITY. . . . put 'em away . . .

AGNES. Yes . . .

FELICITY. Put 'em away.

VOICE OF INTERVIEWER. All right, then.

(AGNES *turns quickly and goes back into the cottage. The lights fade on the Interview Area. At the same time,* JOE *comes out of the cottage and goes to* MAGGIE, *puts a sweater on her shoulders and kisses her on the head. In the kitchen area,* AGNES *goes to* FELICITY *and tries to comfort her disturbed sleep.*)

FELICITY. . . . Claire? . . . Claire? . . . Claire?

AGNES. . . . yes, Mama . . . I'm here . . . I'm here . . .

(*As the focus shifts down to the porch area.*)

MAGGIE. (*Very quietly.*) I found a picture of us in New York. Kids. We were kids. Laughing. Standing on my head in Central Park. You were in uniform. What did we have? A few days in January was all. A little box camera, and that was broken, it didn't work all the time, you had to be so careful with it.

JOE. You were nervous all the time, you never stopped laughing.

MAGGIE. I was pretty in the picture. I had a head like a rock—headstands, handstands, cartwheels—Remember? I must have been crazy. I could run. I could sing . . . I was in the play one year. The Red Mill.

JOE. You got thrown out.

MAGGIE. I did not.

JOE. You got thrown out.

MAGGIE. No.

JOE. On your ass.

MAGGIE. All right, all right. It wasn't my fault. What was his name?

JOE. I don't know, Vice-principal, somebody.

MAGGIE. Son of a bitch kept putting his hands all over me. (*She almost laughs.*)

JOE. You were pretty.

MAGGIE. I loved it.

JOE. You punched him in the mouth.

MAGGIE. I was scared. What else could I do?

JOE. You got thrown out.

MAGGIE. I got thrown out. (*The words spill slowly as they remember bits and pieces of their life together, searching for some solid ground.*) I was scared. I was still a virgin.

JOE. I never touched you until we were married.

MAGGIE. I wanted you to. I did.

JOE. Your mother would have killed me.

MAGGIE. We went to New York . . .

JOE. Sometimes Connecticut. With Steve . . .

MAGGIE. He doesn't remember . . .

JOE. In the fall, in the Plymouth . . .

MAGGIE. I tell him, but he doesn't remember . . .

JOE. Sundays and Saturdays, when I could get off . . .

MAGGIE. He should have had brothers and sisters . . .

JOE. We couldn't.

MAGGIE. I know.

JOE. They asked me all those questions. I was embarrassed, but I told them. They said, no, no more kids.

MAGGIE. It hurt so bad, I cried . . .

(*In the kitchen,* AGNES *begins to talk to* FELICITY, *who is still asleep.*)

AGNES. Mama . . . mama . . . ? (FELICITY *continues to sleep.*) If I told you the truth, mama, would you listen? If I told you the truth, would you think I was lying?

MAGGIE. (*Continues with* JOE.) . . . I cried.

JOE. I built the house.

MAGGIE. Way out in the country, we thought . . . way out . . .

JOE. Something to *have,* we said. Where does it go?

AGNES. (*Continues to the sleeping* FELICITY.) I don't remember the good times anymore, mama. I keep thinking we have something to go back to. But I don't remember what it is. All I can remember is this . . . this . . .

JOE. Where does it go.

MAGGIE. What a house . . . three bedrooms . . .

JOE. One and a half baths . . .

AGNES. . . . pushing and pulling and hurting . . . this is all I can remember . . .

JOE. I built it all myself.

MAGGIE. The first two years, nothing worked.

JOE. What do you mean, nothing worked? I built it good, damn good.

MAGGIE. (*Gently with a smile.*) The wiring, the roof was bad, the plumbing, we never had water . . . (JOE *laughs.*)

AGNES. It all went wrong. What happened, mama? There must have been a time when I loved you. Oh, mama, if I told you the truth, if I told you the truth now, would it matter?

MAGGIE. Then they put in the sidewalks, the sewers . . .

JOE. *They* never worked, either . . .

(*They laugh. In the living room area,* MARK *is drinking heavily.* BEVERLY *enters from the bedroom where she has just left* BRIAN.)

BEVERLY. He's resting.
MARK. He'll be all right.
BEVERLY. How about you?
MARK. Better every minute. (*He downs another drink.*)
BEVERLY. You could fool me. (MARK *gives her a look.*) Okay. Okay. I'm going. (*She starts to collect her things.*)

(*In the porch area.*)

MAGGIE. More houses, more streets . . . You couldn't breathe.
JOE. Overnight . . . it happened overnight . . .
MAGGIE. We had to build fences. All of a sudden, fences . . .

(*In the living room area.*)

BEVERLY. You're sure he's all right?

MARK. Of course he's all right. It's just this dying business, Beverly. It gets a little messy every now and then.

BEVERLY. I noticed.

MARK. Did you? Brian takes such pride in putting things in order, keeping things in their proper perspective, it's hard to tell. I mean, give him ten minutes and a few thousand words, and he'll make you think dying is the best thing that ever happened to him. Would you like a drink?

BEVERLY. No, thank you.

MARK. It's all words for Brian. And it's a little hard to keep up. One letter follows the next, one paragraph, one chapter, one book after another, close parenthesis, end of quote. Never mind what it's all about.

BEVERLY. That's not fair.

MARK. Isn't it? The way you two have been carrying on, I was beginning to think I was at a wedding. I mean, I enjoy a good joke as much as the next fellow, but dead people are pretty low on my list of funny topics.

BEVERLY. Let's not get angry, we'll spoil your metaphor.

MARK. Fuck my metaphor! It's true! (*Pause. Then quietly.*) My God, listen to me. You think you know something. You think you *have* something . . .

(*In the porch area.*)

JOE. More houses, more streets.

MARK. And it all goes crazy.

JOE. So many goddamn things. Where do they go? The freezer, the washer and the dryer, a dishwasher for Christ's sake, the lawn mower, the barbecue, three bicycles, four, six lawn chairs and a chaise lounge—

aluminum, last forever—the white table with the umbrella, the hammock, the bar, I put that wood paneling in the basement, we finished the attic—well, half of it, I got the insulation in—the patio, with screens . . . Jesus, it was a lot to let go of.

MAGGIE. I don't want to talk about it.

JOE. Before you know it, everything you *had* is gone. Not that it was ever yours but you feel it anyway when it's gone.

MAGGIE. I'm telling you, I don't want to talk about it.

JOE. (*He turns from her.*) Alright! Alright! We won't talk about it.

MAGGIE. You get tired. You get old. My hands got too big. I got too fat. I don't know how it happens, I can't remember.

(*In the living room.*)

MARK. . . . when I met Brian, I was hustling outside a bar in San Francisco. Right after the great 'summer of love.' You remember the summer of love . . . one of those many American revolutions that get about as far as Time Magazine and then fart to a quick finish. Well, just after the summer of love, winter came. Which was the last thing anybody expected. And suddenly it got very cold. People were starving to death in the streets.

BEVERLY. Sounds lovely.

MARK. Very colorful—you would have liked it. Anyway, like everybody else, I was very hungry, very desperate . . . the whole scene. So there I was one night, like many other nights, selling it down on Market Street, I wasn't very good at it, but it was paying the rent, and Brian walks up to me . . . I didn't know him of course . . . he walks up and asks me the *time*. Right? Well, I did my little number about time for what and how much was it worth to him . . . I figured anybody who'd come on to me with an old line like that was good for a fast twenty. And all of a sudden, he starts explaining exactly what time *was* worth to him . . . Philosophy! On Market Street. And before I know it, he's into concepts of history, cyclical and lineal configurations, Hebraic and Greco-Roman attitudes, repetitive notions . . . time *warps*, even! Jesus, I thought, I've got a real freak on my hands!

BEVERLY. You did.

MARK. And he's talking and talking and talking and I'm thinking I've got to score soon because it's getting late and I need the bread and I'm hungry . . . but I can't get *rid* of him. I walk away, and he walks away *with* me. I go inside the bar and *he* goes inside the bar. A real 'fuck bar.' I figured this has got to shake him. Right? Nothing. He didn't even *notice*. People are humping on the tables practically and he's quoting Aristotle to me and Whitehead and elaborating on St. Thomas Aquinas' definition of sin . . . completely oblivious to everything around him! I thought I was losing my mind. Finally, I said, 'Look, man, I haven't eaten in a long time, and I'm getting a headache. Why don't we talk some business before I starve to death?'

BEVERLY. What did he do?

MARK. He bought me dinner! I couldn't believe it. I mean, what the hell did he *want* from me? And he never stopped talking. Never.

BEVERLY. Perfect. And then he left.

MARK. Right.

BEVERLY. He didn't want *anything* from you.

MARK. But before he went, I lifted his wallet.

BEVERLY. I always warned him not to talk to strangers.

MARK. It doesn't matter, because the next day I returned it. I don't know why. I just did. And that's how I got to know him. I got interested in what he was doing . . . which as it turns out was nothing. But he was doing it so well. He gave me a room. I could use it whenever I wanted. I started reading again . . . I thought to myself, my god, I could really *do* something. Salvation! We talked and talked endlessly . . . word equals idea equals action equals change equals time equals freedom equals . . . well, who knows? But the point is . . . I don't know what the point is. What am I talking about?

BEVERLY. Dead people.

MARK. Exactly! I mean, exactly!

BEVERLY. Exactly what?

MARK. I mean *it's not enough!* Ten thousand pages of paragraphed garbage . . . it's just words. We are dying here, lady. That's what it's about. Brian looks at me and I can see it in his eyes. One stone slab smack in the face, the rug is coming out from under, the light is going *out*. You can do the pills and the syringes and the "let's play games" with the cotton swabs and x-rays, but it's not going to change it. You can wipe up the mucous and the blood and the piss and the excrement, you can burn the sheets and boil his clothes, but it's still there. You can smell it on him. You can smell it on me. It soaks into your hands when you touch him. It gets into your blood. It's stuck inside him, filling up inside his head, inside his skin, inside his mouth. You can taste it on him, you can swallow it and feel it inside your belly like a sewer. You wake up at night and you shake and you spit. You try to vomit it out of you. But you can't. It doesn't go away. It stays inside you. Inside every word, every touch, every move, every day, every night, it lies down with you and gets in between you. It's sick and putrid and soft and rotten and it is killing me.

BEVERLY. It's killing him, too.

MARK. That's right, lady. And some of us have to watch it. Some of us have to live with it and clean up after it. I mean, you can waltz in and out of here like a fucking Christmas tree if you want to, but some of us are staying. Some of us are here for the duration. And it is not easy.

BEVERLY. And some of us wouldn't mind changing places with you at all.

MARK. And some of us just don't care anymore.

BEVERLY. What?

MARK. Some of us just don't care.

BEVERLY. You're cute, Mark. But next to me, you are the most selfish son of a bitch I've ever met.

MARK. Oh, wonderful! That's what I needed. Yes, sir. That's just what I needed.

BEVERLY. You're welcome.

MARK. Look, don't you think it's time you picked up all your little screwing trophies and went home?

BEVERLY. Past time . . . way past time. The sign goes up and I can see 'useless' printed all over it. Let me tell you something, as one whore to another—what you do with your ass is your business. You can drag it through every gutter from here to Morocco. You can trade it, sell it, or give it away. You can run it up a flagpole, paint it blue or cut it off if you feel like it.

I don't care. I'll even show you the best way to do it.
That's the kind of person I am. But Brian is different.
Because Brian is stupid. Because Brian is blind. Because Brian doesn't know where you come from or
who you come from or why or how or even what you
are coming to. Because Brian happens to need you.
And if that is not enough for you, then you get yourself out of his life—fast. You take your delicate sensi-
bilities and your fears and your disgust, if that's all
you feel, and you pack it up and you get out.

MARK. That simple, huh?

BEVERLY. Yes. That simple. A postcard at Christmas,
a telegram for his birthday, and maybe a phone call
every few years . . . if he lives. But only when it gets
really bad. When the money and the time and the
people are all running out faster than you care to
count, and the reasons don't sound as good as they
used to and you don't remember anymore why . . .
why you walked out on the one person who said yes,
you do what you have to because I love you. And you
can't remember anymore what it was you thought you
had to do or who the hell you thought you were that
was so goddamn important that you couldn't hang
around long enough to say goodbye or to find out what
it was you were saying goodbye to . . . Then you
phone, because you need to know that somewhere, for
no good reason, there is one poor stupid deluded
human being who smells and rots and dies and still
believes in you. One human being who cares. My God,
why isn't that ever enough?

MARK. You want an answer to that?

BEVERLY. No. I want you to get yourself together
or get yourself away from him.

MARK. Just leave.

BEVERLY. Yes.

MARK. I can't.

BEVERLY. Why not?

MARK. He's dying.

BEVERLY. He doesn't need *you* for that. He can do it all by himself. You're young, intelligent, not bad looking . . . probably good trade on a slow market. Why hang around?

MARK. I can't leave him.

BEVERLY. Why not?

MARK. I owe him.

BEVERLY. What? Pity?

MARK. No.

BEVERLY. Then what? What?! You don't make sense, Mark. I mean, what's in it for you?

MARK. Nothing's in it for me.

BEVERLY. You said it yourself. He's just a tired, sick old man . . .

MARK. I didn't say that.

BEVERLY. . . . A tired old trick with some phony ideas that don't hold piss, let alone water . . .

MARK. What?

BEVERLY. A broken-down sewer, that's all he is.

MARK. I didn't say that . . .

BEVERLY. Yes, you did. Garbage. You don't need that. You don't need to dirty your hands with that kind of rotten, putrid filth. 'Unless of course you need the money. What does he do—pay you by the month? Or does it depend on how much you put out.

(MARK *suddenly hits her in the face.* BEVERLY *quickly slaps him back—hard.* MARK *is stunned.* BEVERLY *hits him again.* MARK *still doesn't move. Almost as if he doesn't feel anything.* BEVERLY *continues to slap his face until he connects with the pain. He lets out a pure cry and breaks down.*)

MARK. I don't want him to die. I don't . . . Please
. . . (BEVERLY *puts her arms around him.*) I don't
want him to die.

(JOE *is at Up Left.* MAGGIE *is at Up Right.*)

JOE. Maggie . . . ?
MAGGIE. (*Crossing to Up Left.*) I'm here, Joe. It's
all right.
JOE. Maggie . . . ?

(*In the kitchen area.*)

FELICITY. Claire . . . ?
AGNES. Yes, mama . . .

(*The lines overlap, coming from all three areas.*)

MAGGIE. I'm here, Joe . . .
BEVERLY. It's all right . . .
FELICITY. Claire . . . ?
AGNES. Yes, mama . . . I'm here . . .
MAGGIE. It's all right now . . .
BEVERLY. It's all right.
AGNES. It's all right . . .
MAGGIE. Sshhh . . .
BEVERLY. It's all right. It's all right.
MAGGIE. Sshhh . . . (*Pause.*)
BEVERLY. (*Gently.*) Hopes, baby. That's what you
got. A bad case of the hopes. They sneaked up on you
when you weren't looking. You think maybe it's not
gonna happen. You think maybe you'll find some way
out. Some word that's still alive, some word that will

make it all different . . . Maybe, maybe, maybe . . .

FELICITY. (*Waking up.*) Claire . . . ?

MAGGIE. It's all right . . .

AGNES. Yes, mama . . .

MAGGIE. Sshhh . . .

BEVERLY. Please, baby. Just one favor you owe him. Don't hurt him. Don't hurt him with your hope. (MARK *pulls away from* BEVERLY.) He needs somebody. (MARK *doesn't answer.*) Yeah. That was my answer, too. (*She gathers her things.*) 'Bye, baby.

MARK. Wait . . .

BEVERLY. No, no. Another two minutes and I'll be dancing you all over the floor.

MARK. I might not mind.

BEVERLY. Might not mind? You'd love it.

MARK. All right. I'd love it.

BEVERLY. Tell Brian goodbye for me.

MARK. Don't you want to see him?

BEVERLY. No. I've got a plane to catch. I want to get to Hawaii before the hangover hits me. (*She stops and turns to* MARK.) It's funny, he always makes the same mistake. He always cares about the wrong people.

(*In the kitchen area.*)

FELICITY. Claire . . .

AGNES. What happened, mama?

BEVERLY. Bye!

FELICITY. Claire . . .

AGNES. You sit down one day, and you get caught . . . you get caught somewhere in a chair . . . in some foreign room. Caught in slow motion . . . (BEVERLY *exits Down Left.*) stretched across the floor, listening to the windows and the doors. It's hard to remember sometimes what you're listening *for*. A whistle, maybe . . . or a shout . . . somebody calling your name. Or maybe just a few words. A few kind words. A ticket to Louisiana . . . a letter . . . something . . .

(*In the porch area.*)

JOE. It would have been nice.

MAGGIE. What?

JOE. A farm.

MAGGIE. We couldn't afford it.

JOE. Some place all our own.

AGNES. Something.

MAGGIE. Just to watch the sunset?

JOE. Every day a different job. Every day a different reason. Something grows. Something . . . all in a day.

AGNES. Something . . .

MAGGIE. It would have been nice.

JOE. Something to have.

AGNES. Something . . .

JOE. Jesus Christ, we built the house, and before we finish, fifteen years, and it's gone.

MAGGIE. We didn't need it. It was more work to keep up than it was worth.

JOE. Maybe . . . maybe it was. But it was *something*, wasn't it? Something to have. You put in one more fucking tree, you fix up another room, I kept seeing grandchildren. What the hell else was it for? Not right away, but someday, you figure, kids running around, falling down under it, when it's grown big enough to climb and you can chase them down, spend some time running around the goddamn house . . .

MAGGIE. (*Still detached.*) The apartment is nice. It was closer to work.

JOE. (*Starting to get really angry.*) Work? Shit. Fifty weeks a year in a flat-wire shop. Twenty-four years.

MAGGIE. We had the saloon in between. And the oil truck . . .

JOE. A bartender and a truck driver in between.

MAGGIE. We *owned* the bar. That was ours.

JOE. Gone.

MAGGIE. And the truck, we owned . . .

JOE. All gone. Christ, even the factory is gone.

MAGGIE. They couldn't get along without you.

JOE. Twenty-four years. Two weeks a year at the beach. One week off for Christmas . . . (*Pause.*) Talk to me, Maggie. Talk to me.

MAGGIE. What? What can I say?

JOE. I don't know. Somebody walks up one day, one day, somebody walks up and tells you it's finished. And me . . . all I can say is 'what?' . . . *what's* finished? What did I have that's finished? What?

MAGGIE. We give up too easy. We don't fight hard enough. We give up . . . too easy . . .

JOE. We got to tell him, Maggie. We got to face it and tell him. Some son of a bitch walks up one day and tells you it's finished. What? What did we have that's finished?

MAGGIE. (*Breaking down.*) Us. Us. For Christ's sake, don't make me say things I don't understand. I don't want to hear them. I shake all over when I think about them. How long? Two weeks? Three? A month? And then what? What have I got *then?* An apartment full of some furniture I can't even keep clean for company, a closet full of some old pictures, some curtains I made out of my wedding dress that don't even fit the windows . . . What? What do I do? Sit down with the TV set every night, spill my coffee when I fall asleep on the sofa and burn holes in the carpet, dropping cigarettes?

JOE. Maggie . . .

MAGGIE. No. I want you to come home. What is this place, anyway? They make everything so nice. Why? So you forget? I can't. I can't. I want you to come home. I want you to stay out four nights a week bowling, and then come home so I can yell and not talk to you, you son of a bitch. I want to fight so you'll take me to a movie and by the time I get you to take me I'm so upset I can't enjoy the picture. I want to get up too early, too goddamn early, and I'll let you know about it, too, because I have to make you breakfast, because you never, never once eat it, because you make me get up too early just to keep you company and talk to you, and it's cold, and my back aches, and I got nothing to say to you and we never talk and it's six-thirty in the morning, *every* morning, even Sunday morning and it's all right . . . it's all right . . . it's all right because I *want* to be there because you need me to be there because I want *you* to be there because I want you to come home.

JOE. Maggie . . .

MAGGIE. Come home, that's all. Come home.

JOE. I can't, Maggie. You know I can't.

MAGGIE. No, I don't know. I don't.

JOE. I can't.

MAGGIE. You can. Don't believe what they tell you. What do they know? We've been through worse than this. You look fine. I can see it.

JOE. No, Maggie.

MAGGIE. You get stronger every day.

JOE. It gets worse.

MAGGIE. No. I can see it.

JOE. Every day, it gets worse.

MAGGIE. We'll go home, tomorrow. I got another ticket. We can get a plane tomorrow.

JOE. Don't do this, Maggie.

MAGGIE. I put a new chair in the apartment. You'll like. It's red. You always said we should have a big red chair. I got it for you. It's a surprise.

JOE. No! It won't work.

MAGGIE. We'll get dressed up. I'll get my hair done. We'll go out someplace. What do we need? A little time, that's all.

JOE. It's not going to change anything.

MAGGIE. No. It's too fast. Too fast. What'll I do? I can't remember tomorrow. It's no good. We'll look around. Maybe we *can* find a little place. Something we like.

JOE. No. This is all. This is all we got.

MAGGIE. No. Something farther out. Not big. Just a little place we like. All right, a farm, if you want. I don't care. Tomorrow.

JOE. (*Angry and frustrated.*) Tomorrow is nothing, Maggie! Nothing! It's not going to change. You don't snap your fingers and it disappears. You don't buy a ticket and it goes away. It's here. Now.

MAGGIE. No.

JOE. Look at me, Maggie.

MAGGIE. No.

JOE. *Look* at me. You want magic to happen? Is that what you want? Go ahead. Make it happen. I'm waiting. Make it happen!

MAGGIE. I can't.

JOE. Make it happen!

MAGGIE. I can't. I can't.

(STEVE *comes out of the cottage.* MAGGIE *and* JOE *look at him.* MAGGIE *crosses away from* STEVE. *He speaks quietly, sensing that he's interrupted something.*)

STEVE. Hey, I'm ready to play for you now. If you want to hear?

JOE. Sure, dad. I'll be right in.

STEVE. It's not great, but it's not bad, either.

JOE. Good.

STEVE. (*To* MAGGIE, *tentatively.*) Mom. I'm sorry.

MAGGIE. What?

STEVE. I'm sorry for fucking around like that. I didn't mean to upset you.

MAGGIE. That's okay.

STEVE. Yeah?

MAGGIE. (*Smiles and goes to him.*) Yeah, yeah, yeah. (*She throws her arms around him and holds him tightly.*)

JOE. You get tuned up, and I'll be right in.

STEVE. Better hurry up before I lose my nerve. (*He exits. After a moment he tunes up and we hear "Goodnight, Irene" being played on the guitar.*)

JOE. I'm going inside now, Maggie. I'm going to tell him.

MAGGIE. Tell me first.

JOE. What?

MAGGIE. Tell me. Say it out loud.

JOE. I'm going to die, Maggie.

MAGGIE. (*After a moment.*) Why?

JOE. I don't know. I don't know. I don't know. Like everything else, I don't know. Come inside.

MAGGIE. What'll we do in there?

JOE. Try. That's all. Just try. Live with it. Look at it. Don't make me do it alone.

MAGGIE. I can't promise . . .

JOE. Don't promise. Just come inside.

(MAGGIE *doesn't move for a long time.* STEVE *continues to play the guitar softly. Finally* MAGGIE *turns and walks slowly toward the cottage.* JOE *joins her and together they walk inside. As they pass through the living room,* MARK *rises from the couch and goes to the bookcase for the Scotch; instead he picks up the tray with the medicine and throws it violently. After a beat,* BRIAN *enters.*)

BRIAN. (*Looking at the mess.*) What happened?

MARK. Nothing. Nothing. I had an accident.

BRIAN. Oh. Me too.

MARK. What?

BRIAN. I need some help.

MARK. What happened?

BRIAN. I . . . uh . . . I fell asleep and I wet the bed.

MARK. Come and sit down.

BRIAN. I'm embarrassed.

MARK. I'm drunk.

BRIAN. Pleased to meet you.

MARK. Sit down. Before you fall down.

BRIAN. (*Starts to sit, but then stops.*) I am truly disgusting.

MARK. No, you're not. Just wet.

(BRIAN *reaches out his hand to* MARK, *they embrace.
    Then* MARK *helps him off to the bedroom. And our
    focus shifts to the kitchen.*)

FELICITY. (*Calling out in her sleep.*) Agnes.

AGNES. Mama, if I told you the truth now, would it matter?

FELICITY. (*Waking up.*) Agnes!

AGNES. Yes, mama?

FELICITY. What . . . what time is it . . . ?

AGNES. I don't know, mama.

FELICITY. . . . sons of bitches . . . Did we get any mail today, Agnes?

AGNES. (*Every word of this lie is now more and more unbearable.*) Yes, mama . . . we did . . .

FELICITY. From Claire?

AGNES. Yes, we did. Another letter from Claire. Another letter from Claire.

FELICITY. (*As if she never said it before.*) I get so lonesome for Claire . . .

AGNES. (*Cutting her off.*) I know, mama . . .

FELICITY. Will you read it to me, Agnes?

AGNES. Yes, mama.

FELICITY. (*Like a phonograph, skipping back.*) I get so lonesome for Claire . . .

AGNES. (*Unable to bear any more.*) Mama, please . . .

FELICITY. I get so lonesome for Claire . . .

AGNES. Please!

FELICITY. I get so lonesome . . .

AGNES. (*A cry.*) Mama!! (*And then silence.*)

FELICITY. Agnes?

AGNES. Yes.

FELICITY. Could I have some tea?

AGNES. (*Almost in a trance pours the tea and carefully puts the cup in* FELICITY'S *hands.*) Yes.

FELICITY. (*Holding the cup, but not drinking from it yet.*) Could you read me the letter, now?

AGNES. Yes.

FELICITY. The letter from Claire.

AGNES. Yes. Yes. Yes. (*She takes the letter from her pocket—the one she was writing earlier. She opens the envelope and begins reading.*) Dear mama, I am writing today from Mexico. We are finally out of the swamp and onto high dry ground. What a relief after so much rain and dampness . . . Because of some unexplainable mechanical difficulties, we found ourselves stranded today in a beautiful little mountain village called San Miguel . . . It's a lovely little town clinging for dear life to the side of a great ghostly mountain in the middle of nowhere . . . a very curious place to be. Nothing has changed in hundreds of years and nothing *will* change, I guess, for hundreds more . . .

FELICITY. (*Mumbling.*) . . . my bright-eyed . . . girl . . .

AGNES. . . . There are so many things to see during the day, but then the nights grow bitter cold . . . (AGNES *watches her, making up the words to the letter.*) and I can hear the wind blowing . . . outside the door, whistling and . . . and whispering . . . and when I look out the window, nothing is there . . . nothing . . . mama . . . I think . . . I think it's because I miss you . . . because it hurts not being close to you . . . and . . . and touching you . . . (AGNES *breaks down and can't go any further.*)

FELICITY. Agnes?

AGNES. Yes, mama. Yes.

FELICITY. What time is it now?

AGNES. Oh, four . . . five . . . I don't know.

FELICITY. (*Still holding her cup.*) Could I have some tea, Agnes? (AGNES *just looks at her.*) Could you read me the letter now?

AGNES. Mama . . .

FELICITY. Could you read me the letter now?

AGNES. Mama . . .

FELICITY. The letter from Claire? (*Pause.*)

AGNES. Yes. Yes. (*She starts to read the letter again.*) Dear mama, I am writing today from Mexico. We are finally out of the swamp and onto high dry ground. What a relief after so much rain and dampness . . . Because of some unexplainable mechanical difficulties . . .

(*She continues reading under the following: In the shadows,* JOE *and* BRIAN *slowly become visible. They are standing in isolated areas, facing the audience as if they were speaking to the* INTERVIEWER. *The coda MUSIC begins.*)

BRIAN. (*Crossing to Down Left stool.*) People don't want to let go. Do they. They think it's a mistake. They think it's supposed to last forever . . .

JOE. (*At Up Right.*) There's a few things—I could talk to you about them . . .

BRIAN. I suppose it's because . . .

JOE. . . . you don't expect it to happen.

BRIAN. You don't expect it to happen to you.

JOE. But it happens anyway, doesn't it? It doesn't matter what you do, you can't stop it.

BRIAN. You try.

MARK. (*In the living room.*) You keep thinking, there's got to be some way out of this.

BRIAN. You want to strike a bargain . . . make a deal.

MARK. You don't want to give in.

JOE. You want to say no.

MAGGIE. (*At Up Right.*) . . . no . . .

MARK. . . . no . . .

BRIAN. Your whole life goes by—it feels like it was only a minute.

BEVERLY. (*Entering Stage Left and moving to the Left porch.*) You try to remember what it was you believed in.

MARK. What was so important?

MAGGIE. What was it?

BEVERLY. You want it to make a difference.

MAGGIE. You want to blame somebody.

BRIAN. You want to be angry.

JOE. You want to shout, 'Not me!'

BRIAN. Not me!

MAGGIE. Not me!

FELICITY. What time is it, Agnes?

AGNES. I don't know, mama.

BRIAN. And then you think, someone should have said it sooner.

MARK. Someone should have said it a long time ago.

BEVERLY. When you were young.

BRIAN. Someone should have said, this living . . .

MARK. . . . this life . . .

BEVERLY. . . . this lifetime . . .

BRIAN. It doesn't last forever.

MAGGIE. A few days, a few minutes . . . that's all.

BRIAN. It has an end.

JOE. Yes.

MARK. This face.

BEVERLY. These hands.

MARK. This word.

JOE. It doesn't last forever.

BRIAN. This air.

MARK. This light.

BRIAN. This earth.

BEVERLY. These things you love.

MAGGIE. These children.

BEVERLY. This smile.

MAGGIE. This pain.

BRIAN. It doesn't last forever.

JOE. It was never supposed to last forever.

MARK. This day.

MAGGIE. This morning.

BEVERLY. This afternoon.

MARK. This evening.

FELICITY. What time is it, Agnes?

AGNES. I don't know, mama. It's time to stop. Please, mama. It's time to stop.

BRIAN. These eyes . . .

MARK. These things you see.

MAGGIE. It's pretty.

JOE. Yes.

MARK. Yes.

BRIAN. These things you hear.

MARK. This noise.

BEVERLY. This music.

STEVE. I can play for you now. It's not good, but it's not bad either.

MAGGIE. Yes.

BEVERLY. Yes.

BRIAN. They tell you you're dying, and you say all right. But if I *am* dying . . . I must still be alive.

FELICITY. What time is it?

MARK. These things you have.

MAGGIE. Yes.

JOE. This smell, this touch.
MARK. Yes.
BEVERLY. This taste.
BRIAN. Yes.
MAGGIE. This breath.
STEVE. Yes.
MARK. Yes.
BRIAN. Yes.
MAGGIE. Yes.
BEVERLY. Yes.
JOE. Yes.
BRIAN. This moment. (*Long pause. Lights fade.*)

END OF PLAY

PROPERTY LIST

ONSTAGE
Kitchen Area
in table drawer
    envelope, stamped & addressed to:
      (destroyed each night)   Mrs. Felicity Thomas
                          City of Hope
                          Mendocino, Calif. 90024

    2 ballpoint pens
    stationery
    calendar diary
Agnes' chair square with table
on cabinets and stove
    tea kettle with light tea on s.r. burner
    tea pot—full of light tea
    loose tea in canister
    glass with water
    blue basin with water
    washcloth
    lava soap
    blue bottle with water
    mug with silver and utensils (dressing)
    sewing basket with needlepoint (check yarn)
    checker board and checkers
    pill tray with assorted pill bottles (Gelatin)
    box of Kleenex
above s.r. shelf
    salt and pepper shakers
    creamer
    sugar bowl

2 calibrated shot glasses
glass measuring cup
measuring beaker
4 cups and saucers
above s.l. shelf
  small blue pan
  sugar in jar
  coffee in jar
  rice in jar
  cookies in jar
in s.r. drawer
  4 teaspoons and asst. silver
  rubber gloves (l. side.)
in s.l. drawer
  extra washcloth
in cupboard s.r. (s.l. *side*)
  half round water tank with
    2 tubes (separated)
  K-Y Jelly
  ostomy soap
  odor remover
  box of sponges
brown tray—lower left cupboard
  facing out
2 terry cloth towels on rack
2 pot holders on hook
paper towels (dark pattern)
dressing and filler in cupboards
(never moved)
Living Room Area
on medicine table
  top shelf
    stack of lily cups
    blue water pitcher with water (tape lid open)—d.c.

blue plastic glass—U.C.
pad (marked "every 4 hours") (10, 2, 6, 10)
pencil (on pad)
pill cup (on pad)
tray with
  empirin
  vitamins
  empty pill bottle
  pill bottle with Gelatin
second shelf, medicine table
Kleenex
  sponges
on window seat
assorted spiral notebooks
pillow (brown)
wastebasket by window seat
ottoman to U.S. spikes
swivel chair facing sofa
guitar (tuned) on day bed behind kitchen unit
Furniture
kitchen table (drawer S.R.)
kitchen chair
day bed with pillows
sofa
swivel chair
ottoman
window seat
medicine table
bench D.R.
bench D.L.
bench porch
bench U.L. in woods
canvas chair U.L. in woods
canvas chair U.R. in woods

tree stump U.R. in woods
canvas chair Off Stage (for Act Two)
OFF RIGHT
Maggie
  plastic shopping bag with
    wrapped ham
    purse
    airline tickets (in purse)
    snapshots (in purse)
  brown shopping bag with
    newspaper (New Jersey)
    cookie tin
    pumpkin flowers
    coffee tin
    stuffing
  brown shopping bag with
    crab sauce
    Lysol
    homemade bread in foil
      (rewrapped each perf.)
    jelly (on top)
    peppers (on top)
  large suitcase (empty)
  small suitcase with
    Fanny's present
    jar of clam broth
Steven
  guitar case (empty)
  flight bag with instamatic (side)
Felicity
  wheelchair with
    inflatable donut on seat
    2 pillows (smallest in backpack)
    2 lap rugs

    catch all bag on L. arm with
        Kleenex
        paper cup
  pack on back of chair with
    shawl
    book
    small pillow
    extra Kleenex

OFF LEFT

Mark
  small pill bottle with vitamin C tablets
  glass
  bottle of milk (set at intermission)

Joe
  mug for coffee (fill and set in kitchen at inter-
    mission)

Brian
  spiral notebook with pencil in wire
  apple

IN DRESSING ROOMS

Beverly
  maroon tote bag with
    scotch bottle ½ full tea
    unopened champagne bottle (empty)
    cigarette and lighter
    matches
    noisemaker
    magazines
    container of grass
    party hat
    stuffing (nightie, etc.)

Interviewer
  watch
  file folder

Brian and Mark
  both have watches
  End of Act One wheel Felicity off stage in dark.
STRIKE
  suitcases and flight bag from day room
  guitar case from day room
  checker board and checkers
  clear kitchen table (cups offstage, all else to it's
     preset)
milk out of fridge—set it s.r. for Mark
coffee in mug—set onstage u.l. end of kitchen counter
dixie cup with one swig tea on window seat
noisemaker to window seat
cassette player on window seat (volume off, play button
    on)
  (be sure cassette tape is fully rolled back)
scotch bottle to d.r. end of medicine table (cap off—
    next to)
bloody towels in wash basin (kitchen)
Agnes' chair to Act Two spike marks
K-Y Jelly on nozzle of ostomy pitcher
  exchange empty champagne bottle from Bev's bag,
  with water filled champagne bottle *from offstage*
  and reset on floor next to d.r. end of couch—gaped
  open slightly *(don't* push the cork in tight in champagne bottle)
clear u.r. end of medicine table for milk bottle
ottoman moves d.s. one foot from spike marks
Push Felicity onstage in blackout beginning of Act
    Two.

COSTUME PLOT

Joe
   tan pants
   green shirt
   black shoes, black socks
   brown and black cardigan sweater
   baseball hat

Mark
   old jeans
   cinnamon turtle neck knit pullover
   beige socks
   addidas shoes
   old Army jacket

Interviewer
   tan slacks
   blue shirt
   red and green print tie
   rust sports jacket
   rust jugga boots
   brown socks

Steven
   brown Levi suit, brown wide belt
   blue and red rugby shirt
   white and blue addidas
   white socks

Beverly
   maroon long dress, long sleeves, V-neck
   silver sandals
   slate grey opaque tights

yellow raincoat
black rain boots with buckles
large maroon leather bag

Maggie
shirt waist dress, beige with roses, pleated skirt, long
  sleeves, tie belt
white slip
beige purse
beige shoes
beige tights

Claire
navy blue skirt
blue, red and gold print blouse
beige gold cardigan sweater
navy shoes
beige tights

Felicity
beige and rose print house dress, long sleeves
white slip
black shoes
white wool shawl
blue loose knit sweater
slippers
white Bobby sox and beige tights
brown and beige cardigan sweater

Brian
grey flannel pants
pink shirt
beige and brown ski sweater cardigan
brown loafers
grey socks
handkerchief

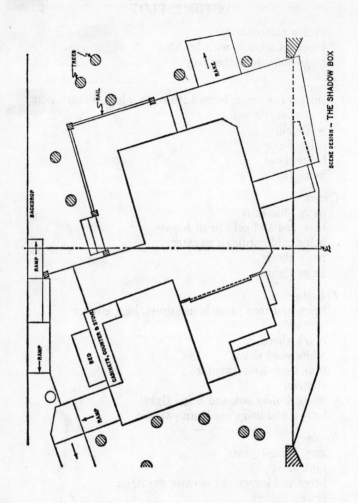

SCENE DESIGN — THE SHADOW BOX